FROM JACK'S JOURNAL

A Novel

HAZIM EL HALABI

iUniverse, Inc.
Bloomington

From Jack's Journal

iUniverse books may be ordered through booksellers or by contacting:

*iUniverse
1663 Liberty Drive
Bloomington, IN 47403
www.iuniverse.com
1-800-Authors (1-800-288-4677)*

*Because of the dynamic nature of the Internet, any Web
addresses or links contained in this book may have changed
since publication and may no longer be valid. The views
expressed in this work are solely those of the author and do
not necessarily reflect the views of the publisher, and the
publisher hereby disclaims any responsibility for them.*

*ISBN: 978-1-4502-4668-2 (sc)
ISBN: 978-1-4502-4669-9 (ebook)*

Printed in the United States of America

iUniverse rev. date: 2/9/2011

To my family and my friends.

This book consists of select pages found in Jack's journal.

The events in the journal were completed with stories as told by Jack's family and friends, as well as police and hospital staff.

January 13, 2010

As told by: David Lee – A senior police officer.

I still remember the day of Sarah's confrontation as if it was yesterday. The memory of it is still stuck in my mind, and it keeps playing over and over again. It was just so crazy and random for something like this to happen in the town where I grew up.

That day, it was slightly snowing, and it was very cold. I was in the station when I received a phone call from a fellow officer reporting a situation that may elevate to a shooting. At first I thought it was joke, because nothing like this ever happens in our town. But my colleague, who had only recently been reassigned to our team, was dead serious on the phone. He even asked me to inform the ambulance service. As soon as I hung up the phone I built a team of officers and headed off to the address that was given to me.

When we reached the neighbourhood, some of the residents were out of their homes; they looked scared but at the same time curious at what was going on. We reached the home intended and stormed out of our cars. There was an older man standing in the garden of the house next door. He told me that a gun shot had

1

already been fired from inside the house. I ordered for the area to be cleared and evacuated and for all the residents to go back into their homes and stay away from the windows. We asked the paramedic team who later arrived to stand at a safe distance until told otherwise.

There was yelling and screaming from inside the house, but I had clear instruction from my colleague not to enter until further notice. Until all of the sudden, everything seemed to quiet down ... It was like the moment of silence that we feel before something bad happens, as if our souls are preparing us for the worst. It was as if my heart was barely beating as I held my breath. A second gunshot was fired, followed by a third. Then silence fell over the house....

At this point, I signalled for my team to storm the house. When we entered, we found a twenty-year-old male bleeding all over the floor and struggling for his last breath. He had brunette hair and hazel eyes, and he looked like as if he had been crying a lot before he was shot. He was later identified as Jack. A little girl about nine-years-old was standing in the corner and was in a state of shock, breathing heavily and staring at him. She had curly brown hair and green eyes. She was later identified as Hailie. On the floor, in the middle of the room there was another girl, but she was about eighteen-years-old. She had wavy brown hair and blue eyes. She held a gun with a strong grip as she stared at Jack. She was later identified as Sarah. My fellow officer, Tom, was lying on the floor next to her and was trying to remove the gun from her hand. He had been shot in the abdomen.

Of course, this has taken longer to spell out then when it actually happened, because in reality, this only took less than a minute for us to scan the room and note the positions of all those that were involved. But as soon as we took control of the situation, I couldn't help but wonder ... This is a bloodbath! What the hell happened here?

*****

The Hospital
January 10, 2010

Three days before the confrontation.

In a very quiet hospital suite, a nine-year-old girl started to slowly wake up. Her hair covered her eyes as she opened them. She brushed her hair away, but her sight was still not very clear. She focused and was able to see a young man and an older doctor standing next to her bed.

She closed her eyes and then opened them again, trying to focus on the young man. He had several bruises on his arms and face. She looked around and saw an older girl, with a white bandage around her head, lying in another bed next to her.

"Where am I?" she asked.

The young man took a deep breath. He looked at the doctor with a strange face and then turned back to her. "You're in a hospital."

She stared at him for a minute. "Who are you?"

"I am Jack. I am your brother ... Don't you remember me at all? We were in a car accident, and you and Sarah were both injured severely. And this is Doctor John, he managed to save both you and Sarah," Jack told her.

"Who's Sarah?" the litter girl asked.

Tears filled Jack's eyes. He stepped closer and sat down on the edge of her bed. "Sarah is our sister. She is the one sleeping on the other bed."

"So what is my name?"

"Hailie … Your name is Hailie."

Hailie tilted her head slightly and watched as the doctor inserted a needle into Sarah's IV. The liquid ran through the tubes and into Sarah's veins. She opened her eyes and seemed to be very drowsy. She looked around and wondered where she was.

Having the same questions as Hailie, she was just about to mutter when Jack interrupted her. "Do you remember anything? Do you know who I am?" he asked.

"No," Sarah replied.

Hailie watched Jack as he looked down and sighed upon hearing Sarah's reply. Then he looked back at John. The look on the doctor's face confused Hailie. She couldn't tell if he was disappointed or if his expression was one of relief that she and Sarah had woken up.

As Jack answered Sarah's questions, Hailie was confused by the feeling of fear rushing through her.

She didn't know why she felt so scared. Something in her heart told her that Jack and John were hiding something. She looked at her arms and legs and wondered why she didn't have any bruises on her body and why her only injury was on her head while Jack's face was bruised. She studied him and noticed he kept pressing his hand against his left side every couple of minutes.

Then she turned to Sarah and looked at her arms; she had no bruises either, but she did have some faded red marks around her wrists. And, of course, the white bandage on her head.

Jack's question interrupted her thoughts. "Are you okay?"

Hailie looked at him. "I am fine."

"Hey, don't worry. Everything is going to be okay now. You need to get some rest so they can let us go home tomorrow." He stroked her hair and kissed her between her eyes. Then he moved over to Sarah and told her the same thing; he told her everything would be okay and that they would pick up their life where they left off before the accident.

*****

January 11, 2010

The next morning, Hailie and Sarah waited for Jack to finish the paperwork for their discharge from the hospital. Dr. John came into their room, and Sarah asked him, "Why do I feel like this?"

"What do you mean? What is it that you are feeling?" he asked.

"I have this mix of emotions that I don't understand; my heart and my mind are very confused," she replied.

John looked over at Hailie. "Do you feel the same way too?"

"I am a little confused but a lot more scared," Hailie answered.

John looked a little worried. He turned his attention back to Sarah. "Well, both of you have lost your memories, and it is not easy for your minds to adjust to the new situation. You had a whole life before this accident, and it's going to take some time for you to adjust to losing the memory of that life. This causes your minds to be very vulnerable, and that is why you might feel insecure or not feel safe, and it is also why you might have a mix of emotions you don't understand."

Jack came into the room with another man named Tom. He was a tall man with dark hair and a well built upper body.

"Everything is ready," Jack said. "We can go home now. The nurses will come now to help you both get ready."

Sarah stared at Tom and then asked John, "Who is he?"

"This is Tom," John replied, "the policeman who was there when the accident happened. This hospital is a couple of hours' drive away from your house, so he offered his day off to give you all a lift back home."

*****

During the silent ride back to their house, Sarah wondered if she would ever regain any of her memories. Would she remember her friends? Would she remember any of her relatives? How would she live with her sister and brother? She didn't remember them. They were like strangers to her. She couldn't help but feel like there was a barrier between them. How long would it take for this to go away? She wondered if—

"Welcome home," Jack said

Sarah's train of thought was shattered. "What?"

"Welcome home. We are here."

"Oh, okay." Sarah looked out of the window and saw a small town. It seemed really quiet, like there was hardly any life in it.

They stopped in front of an average house with an expensive car parked in front of it.

Tom spoke for the first time during the ride, "You go ahead, Jack. Go open the front door and let Sarah and Hailie into the house. I will stay here."

As Sarah walked up to the house, her mind was trying to capture every detail to try and restore her memory. She looked around and tried to recognise any of their home's surroundings, but she couldn't remember anything. The house was grey and seemed to be fairly old with a front garden. Jack opened the front door and asked Sarah and Hailie to go inside. They entered and saw a nice, warm house. Pictures sat on the tables and hung on the walls. The furniture was all new and modern. The home had wooden floors with colourful carpets under the furniture.

"I will go talk to Tom, and then I will show you the way up to your rooms," Jack said.

They hardly heard him. The more they looked at the pictures, the more they drowned in their thoughts. They each picked up a picture. Sarah held one that showed her and Jack sitting in a coffee shop. She smiled. Hailie looked at a picture of Jack carrying her on his shoulders in what seemed to be a theme park. She seemed so happy in the photo. There was something written on the bottom of the picture: *To the best brother in the world. Love, Hailie.*

Hailie stared at the picture for a moment and then returned it to its place. The pictures restored some peace and comfort in the girls' hearts. In the photos, they had both found something they could relate to before the accident, something they could hold on to when their minds struggled to cope with mixed feelings and confusion.

Jack came in and locked the front door behind him. He found Sarah and Hailie lost in the pictures around them.

"Follow me upstairs," he said. "I will show you your bedrooms if you want to rest for a while."

"Where is Tom?" Sarah asked.

"He told me he had to go. He might come back later to check in."

After they went upstairs and saw the rooms, Jack said, "You both can change and rest for a while. I will go out to buy us some food. When I come back and get dinner ready, I will let you know."

Sarah and Hailie couldn't rest at all while Jack was gone. They continued to explore their home as if they were seeing it for the first time. They went into every room and looked at every picture in the house.

When Jack came back and prepared the food, he called them to come downstairs for dinner. During dinner, no one spoke a single word. They sat in silence. Sarah and Hailie both ate, but Jack hardly ate anything off his plate. When they finished, Jack got up and started clearing the table.

"I think Hailie and I will go up to sleep now," Sarah said. "It may have not been a long day, but we certainly need the rest."

Sarah took Hailie to her bedroom and got her into bed. "Don't worry, Hailie," she said. "I am sure that together we will start remembering everything."

She went back to her own room and lay on her bed, but before she fell asleep, she heard Jack walking in the hallway towards his room.

She got up quickly and opened her door. "Jack! Can I ask you some questions?"

"Yes, of course! What is it?" Jack asked.

"How long have we been in the hospital?"

"Just over a week."

"So we had our memories before then?"

"Yes, you did."

"So what were we doing when we had the accident?"

"We were celebrating New Year's." As Jack answered, he turned around, trying to avoid more questions.

*****

January 12, 2010

Sarah was startled around one o'clock in the morning; she thought she heard a sound, but she might have been dreaming. She got out of bed, went outside her room, and headed downstairs to the kitchen. Along the way, she found Jack's bedroom door open. She peeked inside, but he wasn't in his bed.

She continued to the kitchen to get some water, but as soon as she started drinking, she heard Hailie scream. The glass fell from her hand as she rushed upstairs to Hailie's bedroom. When she entered, she found Jack trying to calm Hailie down, but the little girl's screams were out of control. Her eyes were closed as if she was still dreaming.

"Hailie, you are having a nightmare. Please open your eyes and look at me. You are safe. There is no one here that will hurt you," Jack said.

Hailie continued to scream. Sarah sat next to her and held her hand. "Hailie, please open your eyes. Please open your eyes and wake up."

Upon hearing Sarah's voice, Hailie stopped screaming and slowly opened her eyes. "What happened?" she whispered.

"Baby, you were just having a nightmare," Sarah told her. "Jack was trying to wake you up, but you wouldn't wake up. What happened? What were you dreaming about?"

Sarah noticed Hailie staring at Jack, as if she was trying to remember something about him. There were glimpses of fear in her eyes as she said, "I don't remember the dream. It was all so vague."

"I will go get her some water," Jack said.

Sarah waited for Jack to leave the room, and then she told Hailie, "I think you should come to sleep in my room tonight."

When Jack came upstairs, he found Hailie in Sarah's room. He went in and gave her the glass of water. "If either of you need anything, anytime, please let me know. I'll leave my door open. Just call out my name, and I'll be here."

"Thank you," Sarah said. "I think Hailie and I will be fine tonight."

Later that morning, Sarah woke up early while Hailie was still sleeping. She heard someone crying, but she wasn't sure if the sound was coming from the direction of Jack's room.

She got up and walked towards his bedroom, but his door was shut. She placed her ear on the door and confirmed that the sound was coming from inside. She opened the door without knocking. The first thing she saw was Jack sitting on his bed, speaking on the phone while holding a box filled with pictures and cut newspapers. A journal sat next to him.

He jumped out of bed and hung up the phone when Sarah entered. He then tried to collect all the photos back into the box, but Sarah managed to spot one of the pictures before he hid it.

"Who is she? That girl in the picture," she asked.

"That was … umm, that was no one! It's just an old picture of Hailie," he said.

"No! That didn't look anything like Hailie. The girl in that picture looked different, plus she had blonde hair."

"Look, it's really nothing. Please just don't worry about it. Go see if Hailie is awake, and I will go get some food ready for breakfast."

"Can you at least tell me who were you speaking to on the phone? And why are you crying?"

Jack stood silently and stared down at the floor. Sarah didn't think he was going to give her any answers, so she turned around and walked back to her own room, where she found Hailie starting to wake up.

"Hailie, Jack is preparing some breakfast for us. Why don't you get changed while I have a quick shower, and then we will go downstairs to have something to eat," she suggested.

While Sarah was in the shower, she closed her eyes and let the hot water run over her head. She thought about everything that had happened since she had woken up in the hospital. She had so many unanswered questions. Why was Jack crying? Could there have been more consequences to the accident? And what about the picture he had of the little girl? Was it possible she had been with them in the car but hadn't survived?

The more questions that rushed to Sarah's mind, the more she lost track of time until something struck her mind. She opened her eyes wide. Something was missing in all the pictures hanging on the walls downstairs. Where were their parents? How come all the pictures showed only the three of them, without any parents or anyone else?

Sarah finished the shower as soon as she realised she had gotten lost in her thoughts. When she came out of the bathroom, she heard Jack talking to Hailie downstairs. He asked her about the nightmare she had in the night. Sarah dressed as quickly as possible and went downstairs to join them.

She found Hailie looking really troubled and hardly eating anything off her plate. Jack continued to ask her about the nightmare, but she kept replying that she didn't remember.

Sarah went and stood behind Hailie. "Jack, can I have a word with you upstairs, please?" Jack followed Sarah upstairs to her room, and she shut the door behind him. "Is there something that you are not telling us?"

"Something like what?" he asked.

"Was it only the three of us in the car accident, or was the little girl with blonde hair in the picture with us in the accident too? Did she die?

"No! No one was with us. It was us three only! No one died in the accident."

"So what about our parents? Where are they?"

Jack stared at Sarah in surprise. "Our parents?"

"Yes, our parents! Where are they?" she demanded.

Jack stared down at the floor, trying to speak, but all that came out of his mouth were mumbled sounds. Then he took a deep breath and said, "Well, our dad died shortly after Hailie was born, and we lost contact with our mom a while back."

"So that's it? No parents, no relatives, no friends?"

"Look, I understand what you are going through! You are feeling as if someone has pressed a reset button in your mind. So you have all these questions and thoughts rushing in at the same time! But you have to understand that we all went through a lot in this accident. We all suffered mentally and physically. So you should relax these few days and let your body recover first so you can regain your strength. Then all your questions will be answered one by one!"

While Sarah and Jack talked upstairs, Hailie heard the laughter of kids playing outside her home, so she wanted to see if any of them were her friends and might recognise her. She picked up her red winter coat and went outside. She found two little girls around her age playing with their bikes outside the house. She was so desperate to try and renew her friendship with her neighbours; maybe they can help her regain her memory. She went over to them and asked, "Can I play with you?"

The little girls smiled and nodded to her.

"Are you my neighbours?" Hailie asked them.

"Yes we are," they replied.

"Were we friends before my accident?"

The two girls looked at each other and then replied, "No, this is the first time we have met you!"

"But I thought we have been living here for a long time," Hailie said.

"No, you just moved in!" they told her. "One day the house was empty and we were playing in its garden, and then the next day we found all these workers in vans parked outside it, and they furnished it all in one day."

Hailie felt sad and didn't feel like playing anymore; she really needed a friend her age to talk to about what happened to her. So she turned around and went back into the house without saying anything else to the girls.

When Hailie came into the house, Sarah was coming down the stairs after failing to get any answers from Jack.

"Hailie, what were you doing outside?" she asked.

"I just heard the sound of kids playing outside, so I went to speak to them to see if we used to be friends before the accident."

"And are they your friends?"

"No, this is the first time we've met."

At that moment, the doorbell rang. Sarah went and opened it and found it was Tom. Jack came downstairs.

"Can you and Hailie wait here for a moment?" he asked. "I need to have a word with Tom upstairs."

Sarah didn't even reply to Jack. She just stared at him and then turned her attention to the pictures in the living room.

Hailie asked Sarah, "Where were you and Jack talking when you went upstairs?"

"We were in my room. Why?"

"No reason. I just need to go and check something."

Hailie went upstairs to Sarah's room and looked for the clothes she had taken off when Sarah had asked her to change. She looked everywhere in the room but couldn't find them. She went to the bathroom and found that Sarah's clothes were still there. She walked over to Jack's room to ask him about her clothes, but before she knocked, she heard him and Tom in the middle of an argument. She placed her ear on door and listened.

"Jack, I did everything you asked me for so far, but this I can't do. We have already done enough paperwork that could end us up in jail, so I can't add this too. I am sorry, Jack. I can't give it to you."

"But, Tom, please? I was right twice before, and I am sure that I am right this time too! Please. I can feel that something bad is going to happen. So please, just help me once more, and I promise you that I won't ask you for anything else after that."

Fear filled Hailie at their words. She ran back to Sarah's room.

*****

January 13, 2010

That night, as Hailie slept in Sarah's arms, she fell asleep while Sarah stayed awake thinking of even more questions she needed to ask Jack. She had eventually fallen asleep too. The next morning, when Sarah woke up, she found Hailie already awake but still laying next to her in bed.

"How long have you been awake?" Sarah asked her sister.

"I had a dream …," Hailie said.

"I am sorry, baby. I might have been too deep in sleep. I don't remember hearing you scream."

"That's because it wasn't a nightmare. I just woke up and grabbed the bottle of water, but I felt someone in the room, sitting in the corner over there."

"Are you sure you weren't still dreaming?" Sarah asked.

"No, because it was Jack. He asked me if everything was okay. When I told him I was dreaming and just woke up for a drink, he asked me if I remembered the dream. But I lied and told him I didn't, so he told me everything was going to be okay and that I should get back to sleep."

"What was Jack doing in our room?" Sarah wondered aloud. "And what do you mean you lied? Do you actually remember the dream this time?"

"Yes, I do ..."

"So what was it?"

"Jack is not home anymore. He left a little while ago. He told me we shouldn't leave the house until he comes back. So since we are alone, can I please trust you and tell you a few things that are scaring me?"

Sarah sensed from Hailie's voice that she was carrying a burden in her chest. "Yes, of course, sweetheart. You can tell me anything!"

"Yesterday, when you left me to change while you went in the shower, I found some blood in my clothes!"

"You mean you are still hurt from the accident? Are you still bleeding? Where is it?

"Well, the blood was down there! But I am not still bleeding. It looked like it was old blood. I was a little scared, and you were in the shower, so I left my clothes here and went downstairs for breakfast, and I thought I would come back to the room after we finished breakfast and show them to you."

"Okay, can you show them to me now?"

"That's not all what I want to tell you, Sarah! Yesterday when I went outside to speak to the kids playing next door, they told me that we only just moved in! So we haven't been living here for long! And then when Tom was here, I came upstairs to your room, but my clothes were gone! I looked everywhere for them, so I went to ask Jack, but him and Tom were arguing. Jack was asking for a favour while Tom was saying that he has done him so many favours already and that he could end up in jail because of Jack."

Hailie started crying as she continued talking. "I was really scared, so I ran back to your room. I didn't know what to do. Everything around me was confusing, which made me even more scared. I found a number handwritten on one of your magazines, so I called it from your room. I thought it might be someone that we know. But it turned out to be a private number that kids and teens can call and ask for personal help without giving their name or any details. So I didn't know what to tell them, and I just hung up."

Sarah was left speechless. She didn't know what to think anymore!

"All right, Hailie, here is what we are going to do. First of all, when did you last check that you are not bleeding anymore?"

"I just checked when I first woke up."

"Okay, then we need to call this number again, and since we don't have to give out any names or details, we can ask them for any advice and help we need in order to understand the things happening around us. So show me the magazine that had the number, please."

When Hailie brought the magazine to Sarah, Sarah noticed that there was a three digit number (739) written below the helpline number. "What are these three numbers? Did you write these numbers on?" she asked.

"No, I just dialled the whole number above. I didn't know what these numbers were," Hailie replied.

"Okay then, let's just dial the whole number again." Sarah dialled the number.

A woman answered, "Child-line service, how can I help you?"

Sarah didn't say a word for few seconds; she didn't know what to say. The woman sensed the silence as a lack of confidence or fear. "It's okay," she said. "You can talk to me. This line is confidential, and anything you say will not be discussed outside this conversation. You don't even need to give me your name."

Sarah finally built up the courage to speak. "Hello, I have some few questions, but I don't know where to start."

"Why don't you tell me what was the last thing on your mind before you dialled this number?"

"My little sister found some blood in her clothes, and we didn't know what to do."

"Is she close to puberty?"

"No, no. She is still nine-years-old."

"Well, it is still normal for some girls that young to start developing and begin their period."

"But, you don't understand, she is not bleeding any more. It was only few drops in her underwear."

"Oh, I see. Has she fallen or had some sort of an accident that may have caused bleeding from that area?"

"Well, we woke up two days ago in the hospital because we were in a car accident, and we have both lost our memories."

"Oh, I am sorry to hear that. But I think it's best if you take her to a doctor just to make sure she is okay and maybe find out exactly why she bled."

"We don't remember anyone here. We are both really scared, and our brother, who didn't lose his memory, is acting strangely. He is not talking to us much, so we are really confused about everything that is going on."

"I personally don't know anyone who has lost their memory, so I don't know how you must be feeling, but I can assure you that it will take some time for your minds to adapt to your new life. And as for your brother, I am sure he still loves you, but maybe it's taking him some time to get used to your memory loss. I think you need to give it some time before everything will be back to normal again."

"Okay, but as I said, I don't remember anyone here. So I don't know where to go to check my sister."

"Why don't you ask you brother to take her?"

"No! I don't want him to know about this now."

"Is there a reason for that? Do you suspect that he may have hurt her in any way?"

"What? No, not at all. I don't think that Jack would … Wait, can you hold on one second, please?"

Sarah stared at Hailie. She placed her hand over the phone and asked her, "Hailie, you didn't tell me why you lied to Jack and didn't tell him about your dream."

"I will tell you when you are off the phone."

Sarah spoke back to the woman. "I think it's best if I take her alone. I will just ask people outside for the closest clinic."

"If there is anything wrong, you can call me back. Do you have a pen and a paper?"

"Yes, sure, I have one here."

"Write down three, two, five. You can dial this after you dial our number. It's my extension number. This way it will direct you straight to me so you won't have to explain everything to someone else."

"Thank you. I will go now and call you again after I take my sister to the doctor." Sarah hung up the phone and then looked at Hailie. "So what was your dream about?"

"I remember both. I remember the dream I had last night, and I started to slowly remember the nightmare I had the night before. Only, they didn't feel like dreams. I felt that I lived them before. It was something that happened to me before the accident."

"So tell me, what happened in them?"

"The first time, in my nightmare, I was in a house, and I could hear you screaming and crying in a different room. I was crying too, and I was really scared, and I was in a lot of pain. Jack was there too. He was asking me to stop crying. He was swearing to me that he wouldn't hurt me. But I didn't believe him. I was moving away from him. That was when, in real life, Jack was trying to wake me up. So when I heard his voice, I started screaming even more. Then when you came and when I heard your voice, I felt real comfort that you were okay, and I started to wake up."

Sarah held Hailie's hand as she continued to listen to her.

"Then last night, I was dreaming that I was running in a house, not this house, and I was really happy. There was a man sitting on the couch. He wasn't Jack. I knew him in my dream, but I don't remember him now. So I passed in front of him, and I went to the kitchen. I stood in front of the sink to drink some water. But something suddenly happened, and the glass of water slipped from my hand and broke on the floor. This is when I woke up and found Jack sitting in the corner of the room."

"So why did you lie to Jack and tell him that you didn't remember?"

"I don't know! I know he is our brother, but I've got this feeling in my heart that is making me fear him. And every time I catch him looking at me, he always has tears in his eyes. I am scared that something really bad happened either in the car accident or even before it. Something he doesn't want us to remember."

Sarah's thoughts drifted off once more until she finally remembered the box Jack had been holding when she entered his room. She could use the opportunity of him not being home to go and see everything inside the box, including the journal. Maybe there was something written in it that would help them understand what had happened. "I know, Hailie. Let's go look in Jack's room. I think we will find something there."

They went to Jack's room and started searching everywhere for the box until Sarah saw it at the top of his closet. As she reached to pull it down, her heart started beating faster because she didn't know if she could handle seeing what was inside it. She finally grabbed it and placed it on Jack's bed. She sat next to it and then looked at Hailie. "Hailie, I think it would be best if I opened the box alone first …"

"Sarah, the only reason I feel scared around Jack is because I feel that he is always lying to me. You are the only one I trust now because your eyes always tell me the truth. So please, don't ask me to leave while you open the box; otherwise, I will feel that you are trying to hide something from me, just like Jack."

"Okay, you can stay. But whatever we see in here has to stay between us until I figure out what to do."

Sarah took a deep breath as she opened the box, but her hopes were crushed as she saw that the journal and all the pictures were missing from inside it. There was only a gun and few bullets in the box.

"What is Jack doing with a gun?" Hailie asked.

Sarah didn't know how to reply. She stared at the gun and tried to figure out what to do next. "I think we need to focus on what is important first. We should go to a doctor and have you checked to make sure you are all right, and then we should search for some answers to our questions."

Sarah and Hailie got dressed and went outside to try to find the closest clinic. Going out on the streets of the neighbourhood was scary for them. If anything bad happened outside, there was no one they knew who could help them.

Sarah asked for directions from one of the people walking in the street. It turned out that they lived within walking distance to a clinic. It was a house that had been converted to a small clinic for the residents in that area. They went into the clinic and waited in line to see the doctor. Hailie held Sarah's hand and squeezed it every time a nurse came out and called someone's name. Finally, it was Hailie's turn.

They both went in the room, and found a tall woman with short dark hair. She welcomed them and said, "Hello, my name is Dr. Suzanne. What can I do for you today?" she asked.

"Hello," Sarah said. "My sister found some blood in her clothes yesterday, and she only told me about it today. She says she is not bleeding anymore, but I thought it would be best to have her checked to make sure nothing is wrong."

"Yes, sure, I can have a look. But I need some more information before I check her. Is there any reason you think she bled from that area? Has she been in any type of accident the day before she bled?"

"We were both in a car accident on New Year's Eve, and we lost our memories," she replied.

"Oh, I am sorry to hear that," the doctor said. "Do you want me to have a look at any other injuries while you are here?"

"No, it's okay. Let's just focus on Hailie at the moment, and we actually don't have any injuries."

The doctor stared at Sarah. Then she turned to Hailie. "Okay, before we start, I need to make sure that you understand what is going to happen. It is just a harmless check, and it won't take long. If at any point you want me to stop, then you just tell me to stop. Okay?"

Hailie nodded.

While the Doctor checked Hailie, Sarah sat next to Hailie and held her hand. After the doctor finished, she left Hailie in the examination room and took Sarah to the office to have a word with her.

"I am sorry," the doctor said. "This is not really something that anyone wants to hear, but my first impression while I was examining Hailie was that she has been sexually abused."

Sarah broke down into tears. "What? How? Or who could do such a thing to her?

The doctor continued, "I am really sorry again. I can imagine how you are feeling, and I want to assure you that I will help you in every way possible. I will get Hailie all the professional help she needs. However, I need some more information from you. First of all, have you got anyone in mind who could have done this to her?"

Sarah was still crying. After the day that she and Hailie had, this was the last thing she needed to hear. "No, I don't have anyone in mind. Maybe Jack knows something. He is the only one who still has his memory."

"Okay, and secondly, if I ask you to come back tomorrow for few more tests, can you guarantee me she will be safe at home tonight?"

"Yes, of course. She's slept in my room ever since the accident. Nothing will happen to her tonight. But I don't understand how she could have been abused! And who would do this to her?"

"I promise you that I will try my best and give her all the counselling she needs, and maybe in time, we can get answers to all of your questions."

"But can't you find out who did this to her by any of the tests you will carry out tomorrow?"

"Unfortunately, no. From what you were saying about your memory loss, it seems that the abuse occurred before that. Therefore, it is more than seventy-two hours ago, so it would be difficult for us to take any samples or swabs from her that will contain the abuser's DNA. I know this is a lot for you to take in, but I need you to be strong for her. I need you to explain to her what we discussed, and I need you to make her understand what the next few days will be like because we don't want her to suffer more than she already has."

"Okay, I will do all this today, and I will even ask Jack if he knows anyone who could have done this to her before the accident."

"Let's go get Hailie from the room next door, and I will arrange for everything for your appointment to come back first thing tomorrow morning."

*****

The Confrontation

When Sarah and Hailie arrived back at the house, they found Jack and Tom sitting in living room.

"Where did you both go?" Jack asked. "Tom and I were really worried about you. Didn't I tell you not to leave the house when I am not with you?"

Sarah didn't want to say anything in front of Hailie or Tom, so she lied to Jack until she could speak to him privately. "We just went for a quick bite to eat close to here. We didn't know when you would be back, and we were really hungry."

Sarah excused herself and went straight to her room. She dialled the child-line number and the extension number (325) for the woman she had spoken to earlier.

"Child-line service, how can I help you?" the woman answered.

"Hello, I called you earlier today. I am the girl who lost her memory in a car accident!" Sarah said.

"Oh yes, I recognised your voice. Is everything okay? Did you check your sister?"

Sarah started crying once more. "Yes, the doctor said that she has been sexually abused."

"Oh my God, that's terrible. Do you suspect someone in specific that may have done this to her?"

"No, I don't remember anyone. I need to speak to my brother privately and ask him if he suspects someone."

"I don't mean to accuse your brother, but you need to understand that at this point, he is also a potential suspect," the woman said.

"What?"

"I am sorry again. I really don't mean to offend him, but children are abused by strangers as well as by members of the family, so before you speak to him, you need to make sure that you have enough evidence to eliminate him completely as a potential suspect. Because the last thing you would want right now is a confrontation with the abuser."

"No, of course I don't even suspect him at all. I mean he would never—" Suddenly a thought struck Sarah's mind. "Oh my God! He was already there …"

"What do you mean?"

"The night before Hailie found blood in her clothes, I woke up in the middle of the night to get some water, and he wasn't in his room. Then I heard Hailie screaming from a nightmare. I ran to her room but found that he was already there …"

"Look, your mind is very vulnerable at the moment. Every thought can easily change the way you think and can affect your judgments and decisions. You are only saying that because of what I said, there could be a hundred reasons why your brother wasn't in his room when you woke up. That doesn't mean he is the abuser. I need you to talk to your sister and see if she remembers anything else from that night, and depending on what she says, then we can see what to do next. Okay?"

"Yes, okay, I will go and talk to her now."

Sarah hung up the line, and as she was about to walk outside the room, something caught her attention—the magazine that had the child-line number and the three-digit number (739) she had asked Hailie about! Could it be an extension number to someone she had spoken to before the accident? She dialled the number again, but this time she used the three-digit number she had found handwritten on the magazine. Her hands shook, and her heart raced.

A woman answered, "Child-line service, how can I help you?"

"Hello, I found your number written down, and I was wondering if—"

"Oh my God, is this Sarah?" the woman asked.

Sarah felt as if her heart had stopped. "Yes, I am Sarah."

"Oh, Sarah, I haven't heard from you in months! How are you? Is everything all right? Why haven't you called me in so long? I was really worried about you."

Tears started to run down Sarah's face. "I don't know what to say or where to start. But I lost my memory in a car accident on New Year's Eve, and since then, I have been really confused about everything that is happening around me. Please help me."

"Poor you. I am really sorry for what you are going through ... By the way, my name is Annie, and we used to talk all the time. So feel free to tell me anything, and also if you have any questions, I will be more than glad to answer them for you."

"Oh Annie, thank you! I am so glad that I can speak to someone who knew me before the accident. So much is going on, and I really need help ..."

"Sarah, I am like your older sister. You can talk to me about everything that is confusing you. But I must first ask about Hailie. How is she doing?"

"You know Hailie too?"

"Of course, you used to talk to me about her all the time!"

"Well, I just came back from a clinic and the doctor said that Hailie has been sexually abused, and I really don't know what to do. I am afraid it might be Jack because he was in her room in the middle of the night, and the next morning, she found blood in her clothes. But then again, I don't think he could do this to her."

"Oh my God, I can't believe this happened to little Hailie, but ... who is Jack?"

"Jack? He is our brother."

"But you don't have any brothers!"

Sarah was left speechless. "I don't understand. What do you mean I don't have any brothers?"

"Wait, I can't be confused, you must be the same Sarah that I know. If you are, then you should be an eighteen-year-old girl with a nine-year-old sister, and you both live with your father, right?"

"No. Well, everything is correct except that Jack said that our father died shortly after Hailie was born."

"Look, I know your voice. I wouldn't mistake you for someone else. You don't have any brothers, and your dad is not dead. You talk about him all the time."

In a shaky voice, Sarah replied, "But if I don't have any brothers, then who is downstairs with Hailie?"

"Sarah, let me get this straight. You have been told by someone who is *not* your brother that you lost your memory in a car accident and that your father is dead, and on top of that, you are telling me that Hailie has been sexually abused, and you are suspecting that very same person who is the only one that has his memory?"

Sarah started to get really scared. "So what can I do now? I don't know what to do."

"Listen to me, call the police and explain everything to them. Maybe they can come to your house and find out exactly what is going on."

"But there is already a police officer downstairs, and he is telling the same story as Jack."

"So a policeman is covering for Jack? Sarah, what happened to you? I don't understand how you came to be in this situation."

The phone fell from Sarah's hand; she knelt down on the floor and placed her hands over her face as she cried. Her mind couldn't take this anymore. Every second that passed, a hundred thoughts rushed through her mind. She didn't know what to do! How could she get out of this situation? She kept remembering the picture of the little girl with blonde hair. Could she be another victim of Jack's? And what about the argument that Jack and Tom had? And the man Hailie dreamt about, could that be their father? If he was, then what did Jack do to him? Finally, a thought struck her mind—the gun in the box! She could use it to make Jack and Tom tell her everything. And if they tried to harm her, she could use it to protect Hailie and escape from them. She came out of her room and went into Jack's bedroom. She grabbed the box and took the gun and all the bullets. As she came down the stairs, she loaded the gun and went into the living room. Tom wasn't there, but Jack was sitting on the floor, talking to Hailie, who was sitting on the couch.

Sarah stood behind Jack and aimed the gun at him. "Jack, get away from Hailie," she ordered.

Jack turned around, "Sarah! What's going on? What are you doing with the gun?" Jack asked in shock.

"Hailie, get away from here. I want you to go upstairs to my room. I want you to lock the door behind you, and don't come down until I come and get you."

"No. Please, what are you going to do?" Hailie asked.

"I am going to get some answers."

Jack looked at Hailie. "Hailie, please listen to Sarah and go to her room. I am going to calm her down, and everything will be all right. Don't be scared."

Hailie didn't listen to what they told her; instead, she stepped back to the corner of the room.

Jack looked back at Sarah. "Sarah, can you please put the gun down and explain to me what is going on? The last thing I want is for anyone to get hurt."

Tom came out of the kitchen. He had a gun on him, but he didn't even want to think of using it.

When Sarah saw him, she shouted, "Tom, that gun on your back, put it on the floor and come stand right next to Jack!"

"Okay, I will do everything you say, but please calm down. Your mind is in a very dangerous state at the moment, and you have no memory of what happened before the accident, so your mind can be easily filled with paranoid thoughts!"

"Paranoid? Are you saying I am paranoid? Okay, Tom, tell me this: Is it paranoia that the doctor today told me that Hailie has been raped? Is it paranoia that Jack hasn't given me a single answer to any of my questions? Is it paranoia that we came out of a car accident and lost our memories without a single injury or head wound?"

As Sarah talked, her finger started to pull stronger on the trigger until one shot was fired towards Jack. Hailie screamed, and Sarah was shocked too. She hadn't meant for the gun to go off. Tom rushed to Jack and found that the bullet had hit him in the leg. From a distance, police sirens started approaching the house.

"Okay, Sarah, listen to me," Tom said. "If you really think that we done this to you, the police are outside now! You can explain to them everything. Just put your gun down before anyone else gets shot."

"No, I need to know some answers from Jack. Jack, tell me, who is the girl in the pictures? Did you rape her too?"

Jack started to cry. "What? Me? Rape her? No, I didn't! Sarah, you have no idea what is going on. Please just put the gun away, and I will explain everything to you."

"No. I don't want to hear anymore lies. I am sick of hearing *lies!*" Sarah aimed the gun towards Jack's chest. This time, they knew she wouldn't miss.

Jack stood up on his wounded leg, still crying. He spoke in a voice filled with a lot of pain. "Okay, okay, I will tell you everything. I swear there will be no more lies. The girl in the picture, her name is Lily. She was my little sister, but she is dead now. You and Hailie weren't in a car accident. Your memories were erased by a specialised doctor. And … and … the truth is I am not your brother. But I swear to you, I never hurt—"

Sarah shot Jack in the chest. Tom jumped towards her to push her away before she could shoot Jack a third time, but as he did so, another shot was fired. Tom and Sarah lay on the floor. Tom rolled over. He had been shot in the abdomen.

Hailie didn't scream. She was left in shock, staring at Jack, while Sarah and Jack's eyes were locked. The police officers knocked the door down and entered. The senior officer saw Tom on the floor, trying to remove the gun from Sarah's hand. He knelt down and helped Tom remove it.

After they secured the area, they called for the paramedics to resuscitate Jack. Sarah saw him giving away his last breath trying to mumble something to her.

The police officers took Sarah and Hailie outside. Sarah was still in shock; she didn't fully comprehend yet what had just happened and what all the things that Jack said meant. Her mind wished Jack wouldn't survive, but her heart blamed herself for what she had done and hoped they could bring Jack back to life.

A paramedic came out of the house, helping Tom walk. Tom came up to Sarah, tears filling his eyes. "You shot Jack right in the chest when he was just about to explain to you everything that happened."

*****

The Florist
January 20, 2010

The next week felt like a movie in fast-forward for Sarah and Hailie. They spent the first two days between the police station and the hospital and a few hours in a counselling session.

Sarah felt hypnotised the whole time. She felt present in her body, but her mind was totally absent. She felt as if everything around her was passing by while she stood still.

They were finally sent home but with no information about Jack or anything. It was as if nothing had happened at all. Sarah didn't have the strength to ask any more questions. Look what had happened the last time she had tried to find out some answers.

Hailie's dreams and nightmares continued every night. The more she dreamt, the more she started getting closer to what happened before she lost her memory. But she couldn't share what she started to remember with Sarah because Sarah hadn't spoken a word to her in a week.

Wednesday marked an entire week since Sarah had confronted Jack. She sat on the couch reminiscing. Last Wednesday, around the same time, she had shot him while he was explaining what he had done …

Suddenly the doorbell rang. Sarah walked over to the front door and opened it. An older woman with grey hair stood there smiling.

"You must be Sarah," the woman said. "I am the florist, a friend of Jack's. May I please have a word with him? Is he in?"

Sarah took a step back silently, to allow the woman to come in as she tries to think of words to reply to her question.

"No, Jack is not in. He was shot last week."

"What? When? He came to see me last week when he gave me his journal"

"You have Jack's journal?"

"Yes I do, but please tell me what happened to him? How did it happen?"

"Can you please just give me his journal; I need to know what is going on." Sarah told her.

"I will, but first please tell me Sarah, what happened to him?"

Sarah started crying, "Look, stop saying my name and pretending to know me. You don't know me, and you don't know what I have been through, or what

Jack has done to me and Hailie. So please just tell me where is Jack's journal. Because you don't know what it's like inside my head, and I can't take any of this any more. So I want to find out everything before you start adding to my confusion."

The woman pulled out Jack's journal from her bag. "Here it is! I am sorry Sarah, but the fact is, I do know exactly what you are going through. So you can take it to read it, and I will go to the police and find out exactly what happened to Jack."

Sarah took the journal and sat on the couch, as the florist was about to open the front door to leave, Sarah whispered, "Please don't leave me."

The florist turned around and saw Sarah still crying with her shaky hands holding the closed journal. Sarah continued to talk. "I don't know what is written inside this journal, but I am sure it will have things that my mind will not be able to handle. I don't know anyone else, and I am really scared. Can you please stay with me when I read it? I don't want to be alone."

The florist walked over to Sarah and sat next to her. She took the journal and placed it on the table in front of them.

"I will stay with you Sarah, and since I am here, I might as well start Jack's story from the where it matters, not from where his journal begins. I promise you that when I finish what I have to say, there will be no more unanswered questions. Is that okay with you?"

Sarah was overwhelmed with feelings. "Yes, please! You have no idea how much I need answers."

"Okay then. Let me start Jack's story. It all began one day before Lily started school ..." the florist said.

Sarah couldn't believe her ears when she heard the florist say the name *Lily*. This is the name that Jack mentioned right before she shot him.

*****

Lily
September 14, 2008

Jack was in the kitchen of a very expensive house, preparing dinner. His little sister, Lily was sitting on the couch, she was six-years-old with short blonde hair. He came out of the kitchen with two plates. "Food is ready," he said. "I got your favourite animated movie, and I got some snacks to eat after dinner."

"I still don't want to go to school." Lily insisted.

"I know you don't want to, but you and I have been home all year. You need to start school! You will still see me all the time because I will always be the one who will take you to school and bring you back home. So you will only be without me for few hours in the morning, then we will spend the rest of the day together."

"But why can't you come with me to school?"

"Because they won't let me! And I have to start university too. I am one year late for my studies just like you."

The front door of the house opened, and their mom, Laura, came in. She had short red hair and no make up on. Her eyes always showed tiredness and exhaustion. She walked over to the living room and kissed them both.

"There is still hot food left, Mom, if you are hungry," Jack said.

"No, that's okay, I already ate. I am just going to have a bath and go to bed. Can you please make sure Lily goes to bed after dinner? You don't want her to be sleepy on her first day in school."

"Actually, I told her because it's her last day before school, I will let her have some snacks and stay up until the end of the movie."

Laura smiled at Jack. As she was headed towards her room, she said, "Will you ever stop spoiling her? Good night, kids."

By the time the movie ended, Lily was already sleeping with her head resting on Jack's leg. He switched off the TV and carried her to her bed. He tucked her in and kissed her between her eyes. Then he went to his own room. He sat at his desk and started reading a book. A couple of minutes later, Lily came into his room and went straight to his bed. She climbed under the covers. "Why did you put me in my bed?"

He smiled as he got up from his chair. He came and lay down next to her.

"It has been a year, Lily. Don't you think it's time you slept in your own bed?"

Lily replied softly from underneath the covers, "No, not yet."

*****

The next morning, Jack lay in his bed. For some reason, he hadn't been able to get any sleep all night. He kept watching his alarm clock as it got closer and closer to the time he had set it for the night before. As soon as the alarm went off, he turned it off and started waking Lily up. But she didn't want to wake up; she was too tired to get up this early. He carried her to the bathroom, poured some water in his hands, and wiped her face with it to help her wake up. "Okay, use the toilet while I go get your clothes ready."

He went to her room and prepared all the clothes for her first day in school.

Lily walked into the room. "I am not feeling well. I don't want to go to school today."

Jack smiled. "Come on, Lily, you are just saying that because it's your first day in school, but believe me, this feeling will go away once you actually start it and meet your new friends. Now come here so I can dress you."

"No, please. I don't want to go today. Can I go tomorrow instead?"

"Lily, it's only few hours, and I will come pick you up. Don't worry. You will have a great day there."

Laura came into the room and gave Lily a kiss. "I am off to work, baby. Have a great day at school, and I will see you tonight."

Jack dressed Lily and took her to the kitchen to prepare her a lunch pack, and then they went outside to his luxurious car.

On the way to school, Jack stopped at a traffic light.

"How come it's really quiet?" Lily asked.

"That's because we are really early. You have never seen the streets this early before, but don't worry, you will see a lot of early mornings from now on." Jack told her.

Just when the traffic light turned green, something smashed into Jack's window and hit him on the head. He felt a sharp, severe pain in his head. And then it all went dark.

With his eyes still closed, Jack heard Lily screaming and calling his name. He tried to open his eyes, but his mind was still trying to grasp what happened. He finally managed to open his eyes, but everything around looked so blurry.

He tried to move, but he realised his hands were tied behind his back to a pipe.

"Lily … Lily, where are you? I can't see properly! Lily? Answer me, please!"

Lily continued to scream. She couldn't hear his voice. He kept focusing his sight until everything became much clearer. He seemed to be in an abandoned warehouse. Two people were going through his car, but Lily was not with them. He could hear her voice in a room close to him. Her cry became so much sharper. He could hear that she was in so much pain. "Lily! Please, leave her alone!"

He struggled forcefully to try to release his hands, but the rope was wrapped too tightly around them. The more Lily screamed, the more he struggled to release himself. He made a sudden move that caused his left shoulder to dislocate. Despite the pain it caused him, he didn't feel a thing. He felt something else when he pulled his shoulder out of its socket. He felt his hand freeing from the rope.

He quickly untied his second hand and ran towards the room where he could hear Lily crying, but the two men that were going through his car saw him, jumped on him, and brought him to the ground.

He fought them with every last bit of energy he had until he suddenly stopped. As the two men continued to kick and punch him, he stared towards the room where Lily was being held. He could no longer hear her screams.

One of the two men hit Jack on the head once again using the same object he had hit him with in the car. Jack fell unconscious again.

"Sir," a muted voice said. "Sir, can you hear me?"

Jack slowly opened his eyes and saw a paramedic shining a light at him. There were too many voices and too many noises around him. He could see the paramedic talking to him, but all he could think about was Lily. He struggled to remember exactly what had happened. When everything finally connected in his mind, he jumped up from the stretcher.

"Sir, please stay where you are. You are okay, but your arm looks dislocated. Please, I need you to stay put."

"Lily. Where is Lily?" Jack demanded. "What did they do to her? Where is she?"

The paramedic tried to hold him down, but she couldn't. He ran towards a second team of paramedics. He found them all kneeling down on the floor. When he reached them, he saw Lily between them, but a police officer came up and grabbed him and started pulling him away.

"No, no. Lily! Please, this can't be happening. Please let me talk to her one minute. I want to see her. Please!"

He fought and resisted the officer until the paramedic came and injected something into his arm. Jack felt his body giving in. Powerless, he fell to the floor.

*****

Once more, he opened his eyes upon hearing a voice. This time, it was his mother. For the first few seconds, he thought it was just a dream. He thought maybe he had overslept and now Laura was waking him up so he could take Lily to school. He was just about to smile at her when he realised he was in a hospital. He looked at his mom, and she looked like she had been drained of tears. "Mom? Where is Lily?"

"Oh, Jack, I am so glad that you woke up," she said.

"Where is Lily, Mom?"

Laura turned her face away. She didn't know how to tell him what had happened. But Jack couldn't wait for an answer. He started to get out of bed.

"No, please, where are you going?"

"I need to see Lily right now. Show me where her room is."

"Jack ... Lily is not in a room ..."

Jack turned around and asked her once more, "Where is she? I need to see her right now."

"Jack, please. I will tell you, but I need you to get back in bed. I can't afford to lose you too. Just get back in bed, and I will tell you what happened."

Jack knew what he was about to hear, but still, every part of his mind was ready to deny it. Every part of his heart was ready to call his own mother a liar just because he couldn't bear what she was about to say. "I am not getting back into bed! Now tell me."

Laura's hands started shaking, and she started to speak softly. "Lily couldn't make it, Jack … She died in the hands of her attacker."

"No. No, she was with me. She was right there in the next room. She was alive just a moment ago. Tell me where she is. I want to see her *now!*"

"Jack, you have been unconscious for almost two days now. Lily died the day you were taking her to school."

"No, Mom. Just stop talking and go get me the doctor. I want to leave now, and I want to go see her."

"Jack, please don't make this harder on me. I lost her too."

Jack's mind couldn't deny it any longer. It tried to find ways of escaping the truth, but it couldn't. He broke down into tears.

"Look, please just get back into bed. I will go get the doctor. He asked me to let him know as soon as you were awake."

Jack got back into his bed while Laura brought the doctor into the room.

"Jack, it's really good to see you awake," the doctor said. "We were starting to get worried about you."

"I am fine. Can I please ask you for a favour?"

"It better not relate to you getting out of bed because there is no way I will allow it in your condition."

"Is Lily buried? Or is her body still in the hospital?"

"No, her body is still here. Why are you asking?"

"Can I please see her?"

"Jack, that's not even an option," the doctor said. "In your state and after what you went through, it will just make your state worse. And as your doctor, my main priority now is to get you better!"

"Doctor, please. I was so close to her. I heard her screaming. I heard her calling my name for help. And then I heard nothing! I didn't get to see her, and now you are telling me I can't even say good-bye? Please, all I am asking for is few minutes. You can even take me on a wheelchair, and I promise you that if you grant me this wish, I will do everything you say, even if you ask me to stay in bed for a month. Please, I am begging you."

"Jack, seeing your sister now will have a huge negative impact on your health. I don't think I can let—"

"Please," Jack's voice became so weak, it was hardly understandable. "Just few minutes with her. She is my little sister."

"Okay, I will see what I can do. But you better start doing what I say from now on. I want you to stay in bed until I figure something out," the doctor said.

Laura and the doctor went outside the room to discuss Jack's situation.

"I really don't think it's a good idea for your son to see Lily's body now," the doctor told her. "It will really do no good for him at all."

"As much as I agree with you, Doctor, I know Jack. He is very stubborn, and he won't rest until he sees her. I think he is in a very strong state of denial, and maybe once he sees her body, he will start accepting the fact that she is gone. And I think he deserves the chance to say good-bye after the way she was taken away from him."

"Okay," the doctor gave in. "I will take him to see her, but if his state gets worse, I don't want to be held responsible for it."

*****

Five Minutes

About half an hour later, the doctor came into the room, pushing a wheelchair.

"Come on, Jack, it's time," he said.

Jack excitedly got out of bed and sat in the wheelchair. As the doctor took him outside and headed towards the level where Lily was being kept, he started talking to him. "Jack, you promised me that if I grant you this wish, you will follow all the instructions I give you. So I need you to listen to what I have to say before you see her."

"Yes, sure, what is it?" Jack said.

"If you feel at any point that you are going to faint, or if you feel that you cannot handle seeing her, it's not too late to turn back. Please let me know as soon as you start feeling unwell when you are in front of her body."

"Don't worry about me. I will be fine. I am ready to see her," Jack said.

When they reached the room where Lily's body was being held, the doctor pushed Jack's wheelchair all the way next to her body.

"Can I please have a moment alone, Doctor?" Jack asked.

"Yes, of course. I will be standing outside. If you wish, you can uncover her face, but please don't forget your promise. Anytime you feel unwell, just let me know. I will leave you alone for five minutes," the Doctor said before he left the room.

Jack remained seated in the wheelchair. He hadn't come to say good-bye. He had only come because there was still a part of him that was in denial, a part of him that didn't believe that Lily was really gone. Something inside him was still convinced that the body in front of him was not Lily. But now that he was in front of her body, he began to doubt he had the strength to uncover her face to find out for sure. He stood up, pushed the wheelchair back, took a deep breath, and grasped the white sheet covering the body. The part of him that was in denial grew stronger, and his hand started to shake. His brain was trying to protect him in a very strange way. He was not there to identify the body. He was not there because his sister was missing and they wanted him to see if this was her body or not. He was only there to say good-bye. There was no chance that it was not Lily. But he didn't think about all of that. He only wished that when he uncovered the face, he would see someone else, as if the hospital had made a mistake all along. He removed the sheet covering the body's face and there she was … Lily. His legs couldn't carry him anymore. He fell to the floor and broke down into tears. He cried because his mind could no longer deny what had happened. He started playing back her screams and her cries. He felt the sharpness of her cry in his ears, and he could still hear her calling his name to come and save her.

He didn't have the strength to stand up again, so he reached up with his hand and held Lily's hand. He pulled it down slowly until her hand was in front of his face. As he held it, he continued to cry.

"I am really sorry that I couldn't save you, Lily. I tried my best. I swear I did. When I heard you screaming, I did my best to untie myself, and I ran towards you, but the two guys kept beating me. I fell to the ground, and they still kept beating me until I fell unconscious. I am really sorry ..., I never thought you would be taken away from me ... I never even imagined your day would come before mine. And I never thought that this is how it would end for you. I know you are in a better place now. And if you could hear me, then please know that I did my best. And that I—"

Jack suddenly stopped talking. He hadn't noticed that while he was talking, a part in his mind had been born, a part of his mind that would haunt him forever, a part of his mind that blamed himself for what happened.

He then continued talking. "*No!* Maybe if I had done my best, you would still be alive.

My stupid body gave up on me, and I fell unconscious just because I was being kicked and punched while you were going through so much more pain. Yet you stayed conscious the whole time and kept screaming for me to come and help you. Your mind kept you awake so I could come and save you … But I didn't. If you can really hear me, Lily, I am sorry I let you down. I am sorry I didn't answer your cries. I hope you can forgive me. Please forgive me, Lily."

Jack kissed Lily's hand, and was about to slowly place it next to her body, when he noticed the tag attached to a small paper onto her hand. It had the cause of death written on it. Jack didn't want to look, but he couldn't resist. He needed to know how and why he lost Lily forever. He turned the piece of paper, and as soon as he read what was written on it, his face froze.

The doctor waited outside for another couple of minutes before he entered. When he saw Jack on the floor, he ran to him. "Jack, what happened?"

He helped Jack stand up, but Jack was still holding tight to Lily's hand.

"Hey, can you please let go of her hand?"

Jack looked at the doctor, and then he looked back at Lily. He placed her hand under the sheet again, and he leaned forward and kissed her between her eyes. Then he covered her face.

*****

Jack spent a week in the hospital after he saw Lily. But he kept his promise and obeyed all the doctor's orders. However, he didn't speak to anyone, not even his mother. He used to only listen to the doctor's orders without saying anything back. When the week was over, Jack got ready to leave while the doctor and Laura spoke outside the room. "Here is a number to a friend of mine," the doctor said. "If you feel that Jack is still not adjusting to Lily's death, then you need to call this number."

"Who is the number for?" she asked.

"He is a doctor who works in an institute; he will be able to give Jack the help that he needs to get over what happened."

"You mean a mental institute?"

"Well, it's not really for people with abnormalities and disorders as much as it's for people who have been traumatised and have been through more than they can handle. It is very well known, and they will help Jack a lot if he is still experiencing difficulties dealing with what happened."

"So you don't think he will improve by time?" Laura asked him.

"To be honest, I have watched many families say good-bye to their loved ones, but I have never seen someone who reacted the way Jack did. When I went in to bring him out of the room where Lily's body was kept, he seemed different somehow. Something changed him, as if seeing her body shattered the last ray of hope that he had, and reading the cause of her death made—"

"Wait, Jack knows how she died? But you only told me she died in the hands of her attacker, and it's for my best and Jack's if we didn't know exactly what happened to her."

"I am really sorry, I clearly told Jack to uncover Lily's face if he wanted to say good-bye, but I didn't think he will pull her hand and hold it. The tag was on the hand that he held, and the way he looked at it, with his face completely frozen, made me sure that he read it."

"So how did she die? I need to know how my daughter got taken away from me."

"Look, it is your right to find out, but it didn't benefit Jack now that he knows, and it will definitely not make things better for you. So you should at least not find out, so you can help Jack get better sooner."

On the ride home, Jack still didn't say a word. When they arrived at the house, he went straight to Lily's room and stood in front of the door. He looked inside and found everything still where Lily left it. He knew his mom wouldn't go in the room and change anything since Lily was gone, so he went inside and grabbed a few toys that had belonged to Lily and a few of her homemade video tapes and went to the living room.

Laura didn't want to interfere with him; she promised herself she would be as patient with him as possible.

He sat on the couch and started playing Lily's home video tapes. A few days went by with the same routine. Jack did not eat or sleep properly, and whenever Laura went into the living room, she saw him watching Lily's videos over and over again.

One day, Laura came into the room and sat next to him.

"Jack, I am really worried about you. If you don't want to take care of yourself for your own good, then at least do it for me. I lost Lily too, and now I don't want to watch you waste your life away. Please, just go out in the fresh air, eat something, and spend a whole day out. Please, Jack, for me?"

"Okay, Mom," Jack said. "I will go outside for a walk, and I will grab something to eat on the way."

"Thank you, Jack."

Jack got off the couch. He hugged his mom and then left the house. After eating, he took a walk near the shops and saw a little girl around Lily's age standing alone in front of one of the shops. He approached her and knelt down opposite her.

"Is everything all right?" he asked her.

"Yes, everything is fine. I am just waiting for my mom to finish from the shop," the little girl replied.

"You know, you shouldn't stand alone like this in the street. Why don't you go in and stay with your mom?"

"Why can't I stand alone?" the little girl replied.

"Nothing. It's just safer if you are with your mom. But at least make sure you don't talk to any strangers if you still want to stand alone."

The little girl smiled. "But you are a stranger, so why are you talking to me?"

Inside the shop, the girl's mother was paying for her stuff when the cashier asked, "Do you know that man talking to your daughter outside?"

The mother turned around and looked out the shop's window. She saw a stranger chatting to her daughter. Before he stood up, the stranger gave her daughter a soft hug and kissed her forehead. The mother dropped her wallet and bags and ran towards the door. She stormed out and started shouting at him, "Who are you, and what are you doing?"

"Nothing," Jack said. "I wasn't doing anything. I was just asking her why she was standing alone."

"You can't kiss people's kids like that!"

"I know, I am sorry, but I swear I didn't mean anything."

The cashier in the shop asked the security to go and check out the situation.

"What do you mean you didn't mean anything?" the woman demanded.

The security guards reached the mother and Jack. "Is everything all right, ma'am?"

"I was just buying some things, and I saw this man kissing my daughter, and I have never seen him before in my life. Can you please call the police?"

"Okay, ma'am. You stay with your daughter. We will handle it from here."

Laura was sitting at home, when she received a phone call.

"Hello, Ms. Laura?"

"Yes, speaking."

"This is the police. Your son was involved in a situation down in the city centre, and we would like you to come and pick him up, please."

"What happened? Is he okay?" Laura asked.

"He is fine, but we think it's best if you come and have a word with us in the station before we let him go."

When Laura reached the station, she sat down to speak to a policeman before she had the chance to see Jack.

"So what is it officer? What did my son do?"

"Well, your son attacked a security guard after he was accused of acting inappropriately. And by the time we arrived, it was pretty violent. When we got Jack in here, it didn't take us long to find out what happened to him recently and what he has been through. It helped us put some of the puzzle pieces together because everyone was really surprised the way your son easily lost his temper. I think it is in the best interest of Jack, as well as everyone around him, if he speaks to someone about what he went through. Maybe it will help him deal with it better."

Laura sat speechless as the officer spoke; she didn't know what to do to help Jack.

"Can I please see him now?" she asked.

"Yes, of course. I will take you to see him right away."

When the officer took Laura to see Jack, she wrapped him in her arms and sat to talk to him. "Jack, the officer explained to me everything that happened, and we think it is best if you spend some time in an institute that belongs to a really good doctor."

Jack was surprised. "You mean a mental institute?"

"No, not really. It is just for people who have been through similar issues as you have gone through and can't cope with them. This place is to help them deal with it better than they would on their own."

"But I am okay, Mom. It was just a moment where I lost my temper after he was accusing me of things I didn't mean. But I am okay now. I am sure it won't happen again."

Laura couldn't hold back her tears any longer. "No, Jack. It's not okay because the first night you slept at home after you left the hospital, I woke up in the middle of the night to the sound of you crying. I ran to you and found you in Lily's room, sitting on the floor. You were crying, and you told me you were sorry that you lost Lily. You looked at her bed and asked her to forgive you. So I helped you get up, and I took you to your room. I told you that it wasn't your fault she died. And then in the morning, I came to talk to you about it, but you had no memory of it happening at all! And the same thing has happened few times since then. So no, Jack. You are not okay. You need help."

"Has this really been happening?" Jack asked.

"Yes, and you are the only thing left to me in this world, and I want you to get better. I don't want to watch you like this, it's killing me. Please?"

"Do you really think they will be able to make me forget what happened?"

"No they won't. They will just help you deal with it better."

"I promise you I will get better, but please, I don't want to go to any institutes. Can you please just take me home, I can't handle anything that is going on around me."

Laura couldn't help but agree to Jack's wish, because she didn't want to go back home alone too. They both needed each other to get over what happened.

"Okay Jack, we can go home. But I want you to talk to me more; don't let it all build up inside of you. Don't let anger pile up on your shoulders, or guilt to build up in your chest. And most importantly, never let regret take over your heart and slowly infect it with the memories of what happened."

*****

October 22, 2008

As told by: Harry Vine – Psychologist.

I volunteer for the police two days every week. They call me every now and then whenever they need my assistance. That day, on October 22, 2008, they called me and asked me to come and see Jack to decide on his mental stability and whether or not we should send him to an institute.

When I reached the station, I read his file before I saw him, and read that he had already been arrested once before for attacking a security guard. This time however, Jack was walking in the streets with Laura, his mother, when he heard a kid, a little girl around seven-years-old, yelling at a man and saying that he was not her dad. Now in reality, this man was her stepfather, and the kid was just being disobedient, so the stepdad hit her with his hand and the next thing he found Jack pushing him away. The stepdad fell to the floor, and Jack started beating him. Everyone in the street was shocked and some of the people started pulling Jack away from the man. The eyewitnesses' reports say that the little girl was so scared that she even tried to help the people get Jack away from her stepfather.

After the police arrived and controlled the situation, they explained to the stepfather Jack's situation, and guaranteed to him that they will not let Jack go this time without giving him the help he needs, so fortunately for Jack, no charges were pressed against him for the second time.

This is when I got called in, and after reading Jack's file, I asked to see his mom and speak to her about any other information that she might tell me so I can help him. She mentioned that he hasn't spoken much to her since the day he saw the body of Lily in the hospital. He even refuses to tell her what he read regarding the cause of death. When I finally finished gathering all the information, I went in to see him. We sat in the room talking for more than an hour. He looked completely absent, as if his mind is running his memories like a movie playing before his eyes. He was looking at me, but I can see that he watching something else. But he kept apologising for what he had done, he felt really sorry for what he did to the man, and I can see that he was being sincere. But we couldn't let him go back home for his own good. We had to refer him to a specialist who would be able to help him get over what happened.

*****

The Institute
October 24, 2008

Jack came into his room with a nurse. He looked out the window and saw a view of a beautiful lake.

"This institute is privately funded," the nurse said. "It was built in the middle of a reservoir to make sure every room faces the view. Here, you get to engage in any activities you want, and you also get to decide when and where you want your daily session to take place."

"So when will I be seen by a doctor?" Jack asked.

"He will come welcome you any moment now."

The nurse left the room, and Jack sat on his bed. He found a journal and a pen sitting next to it. He opened it and found a sticky note inside it that said, *Welcome to your first session.* Just then, a doctor entered the room. "Hello, Jack. My name is John, and I will be your doctor for the duration of your stay here."

"Hello, Doctor," Jack said.

"You can just call me John! So let us start with a walk around the place just so you can familiarise yourself with the surroundings."

John and Jack went outside the building and started walking alongside the lake.

"How come you have a lake?" Jack asked. "Wouldn't that be dangerous for people who are feeling suicidal?"

"Are you feeling suicidal, Jack?" John asked.

"If I was, then I wouldn't have brought it up to your attention."

"Good! But don't worry about the others. We have our eyes open when everyone is out here. But let us talk about you. Do you want to be here? Or are you only here because you were referred by the police?"

"I was referred by the police, but now that I've seen this place, I think it will be good for me to spend some peaceful time here until I cope with everything that happened."

"That's good so far. We don't like to know that people don't really want to be here."

"But I may be a little difficult regarding the daily sessions the nurse told me about," Jack said. "I don't really think I will be able to sit every day with someone and talk about what I am feeling about what happened. I am just not ready for that yet."

John smiled. "Jack, every room in this place has a journal. Every time you feel you don't want to attend your session, then you should write down your thoughts in that journal. You can take it with you anywhere you go, even if you want to write in it outside by the lake. And we will never ask you to tell us what you write in it. We are only interested to know that you let your thoughts out of your head, whether it is through talking or through writing. However, when you are ready to talk to me, it would be useful for me to know some of the things you have written because it will help me help you more. But as I said, if you never feel like sharing what you write, then we won't ask you to share."

"Thank you, John. I think I will stick with the journal for some time until I am ready for the sessions," Jack said.

"That's all right. So now I know there will be no session today. I just hope you don't stay in your room writing all day. I want to see you outside here with other people. There are many cases here who have experienced difficulties just like you, and I think it would be useful for you to meet them. I will leave you now to have some peaceful time, and I will see you tomorrow."

John turned around and walked away. Jack continued to stand and look out across the lake.

*****

In the middle of the night, Jack was awakened by one of the nurses. He tried to jump out of bed, only to realise he was already on the floor.

"*Jack!* What are you doing?" the nurse exclaimed.

"What happened? You just woke me up," Jack said.

"You were shouting and saying your hands were tied, and you kept calling for help."

"Oh, did I? I am sorry. I don't really remember anything."

"That's okay, Jack. Let me help you up. Do you want me to get the on-call doctor to come and see you?"

"No, I will be fine. I will speak to John in the morning," Jack insisted.

The nurse helped Jack get back into bed, and as soon as he rested his head on the pillow, he fell asleep once again.

*****

The next morning, Jack took the pen and the journal and went outside to sit in front of the lake. He was about to start writing in it when he heard a voice behind him. "Are you going to start writing in your journal already?"

He looked behind him and found an older man, who came and sat next to him.

"Pardon me?" Jack asked.

"I am just saying it's very impressive that you are going to start writing in your journal when you haven't even completed two days here. You must have a lot on your mind. " The man said. "I myself started writing after almost a week of being here."

"What's wrong with starting to write so soon?"

"Well, once you print your first words in this journal, you may no longer be capable of talking to anyone about what you are feeling." The man replied. "I came here five years ago, and I thought by writing in my journal for the first time, I will still be able to attend my sessions. But I haven't attended a single one, and I now have nearly fifty journals under my bed."

"Five years! Why? How much have you gone through in your life that would make five years not enough time for you to talk to anyone?" Jack asked.

"Time is not the factor … but the outside world is. What is your name?" the man said cryptically.

"My name is Jack."

"Well Jack, it's too soon to try and explain to you what this place will slowly start revealing to you. But if you insist on writing in your journal, then you must understand that if you write something that is not real, then it must stay within the covers of your journal. You must never let it out and merge into your reality."

"What do you mean? How could I merge something that is unreal into my reality?"

"As you slowly start putting across your thoughts through writing, your mind will slowly start finding out that for the first time ever, it has no limits. It will discover that it is no longer bound by the laws of sanity and reality. It will let you write what ever it wishes to express. And as time passes you will realise that the life you have created inside your journal makes a better world then the reality you live in. When that happens, you will not be able to differentiate between your fantasy and your reality."

"Is that what happened to you? Is that why you have been here for five years? Are you incapable of finding your way back to reality?"

"No. That is not why I am here. I am only here because I am not as strong as I used to be, so I can't face what the outside world is doing to me." The man said as he stood up. He leaned forward to whisper something to Jack.

"It's one thing to watch your sanity slip away from you, but it's another thing to drain it out yourself because you are too weak to face reality as a sane man!"

With that, the man turned around and left Jack sitting alone by the lake.

*****

From Jack's Journal
October 29, 2008

I have a journal and a pen, and my mind is crammed full of thoughts. Yet I don't know what to write or how to start.

My mind is like an ocean of thoughts, misted with memories and blocked by a dam. I fear that once the dam is gone, my mind will be flooded and I won't be able to keep up. Maybe when that happens, it will be the point where I turn crazy.

I guess if I had gone to my first session with John, he would have been able to remove that dam from my mind without flooding it with my thoughts. But since this journal had a note that said, Welcome to your first session, *I will treat it like my first session.*

Maybe the first thing that John would have probably asked me to talk about would have been about Lily. I still remember the day she was born as if it was yesterday. She was the quietest baby I have ever seen. I got really attached to her to a point where I always preferred to stay home and take care of her rather than go out with my friends. As years passed, she became my whole world. I always planned my day to include her with me in all my activities. And then last year, when Dad died, Mom drifted apart and increased her hours at work. She didn't handle his death very well, and she thought that the only way to stop her mind grieving was to work more and occupy her mind with more duties. I felt I needed to double the attention for Lily. But I didn't know how to make it possible because she already had my full attention. So I moved all her stuff into my room, and for the whole of last year, I became her full-time babysitter. I was there for her twenty-four hours a day, seven days a week. It was all worth it though, because her doctor said he had never seen a child her age cope better after a death of a parent. I knew that even though she loved and missed Dad, I was still able to take away all her sadness and grief.

As I write these words, I still can't believe she is really gone! I keep thinking that I should have believed her and kept her home when she said she didn't feel like going to school. Maybe if I kept her home, she would still be alive now and would have just celebrated her seventh birthday last week. But what was I supposed to do? I really thought she was just saying that to get out of going to school ... I didn't think that her heart was really telling her that something bad was going to happen and that she should stay home. I still hope that when I come out of this institute, I will find her waiting for me at home. I can't imagine going home without seeing her there. But I don't know how long are they planning to keep me here, I just hope that when I want to leave and feel ready to go back, they will let me go.

I haven't told this to anyone yet, but I have been seeing Lily everywhere. Since I saw her body in the hospital, something clicked in my mind, and I've started imagining her everywhere I go. She is always smiling and playing around me.

Does that make me crazy? Or is the man I met today right? Maybe my mind is just too weak to face reality.

November 3, 2008

Jack was walking alongside the lake on his way to his favourite spot where he gotten used to sit. On his way there, he saw the older man sitting alone.

Jack came and sat beside him. "Are we here because we are crazy?"

"Why do you ask?" the man replied.

"Because even before I started writing, I kept seeing someone who is not supposed to be there, so I keep thinking to myself, what if I am in denial? What if they sent me here because I am crazy, but my mind won't accept it, or let me be aware of it"

"Well I have always thought that sanity is a very complicated bliss."

"How come?"

"Because sometimes people hold onto it 'til their last breath, and sometimes they feel that the only way to survive in this world is if they were insane." The man told him. "So maybe your mind is only peeking into the world of insanity for the sole purpose of your survival. Maybe your mind knows that without seeing this person that you keep imagining, you will not be able to survive in this world. And your mind can't afford that, because once that happens; you will travel to the world of insanity with a one-way ticket."

"So we are not crazy?"

"Well, Jack, the outside world, the real world—or, as you may call it, 'reality'—is the really crazy place. Just when you think that this world can't get any sicker, you watch something on the news that proves you wrong! So no, Jack, we are not crazy, because we did not choose to live in denial or choose to imagine seeing people who passed away a long time ago. We are merely people whose minds are too weak to handle what the outside world is doing to us."

*****

From Jack's Journal
December 28, 2008

It's been two months since I came to this institute. I am not doing as well as John had hoped. I haven't written in my journal daily like I was told to do, and still I haven't attended a single session.

John still doesn't know that I see Lily everywhere. I am sure he will think that this is an abnormal thing because I am not coping with her death. And he would want to treat me, but I don't want to be cured. I don't want to stop seeing her!

The nurses still wake me up a few times a week because I keep shouting in my sleep, trying to save her. Last dream I had, I reached a point which I never reached before, I reached the door where Lily was kept behind, and I kept hitting it until it opened. This is when the nurses woke me up. They found me sleep-walking and hitting the door to my room. I don't know what to do anymore. Am I slowly drifting into the so-called world of insanity? Or is my mind just handling it differently than other "normal" people?

John asked me to do two tasks today. The first task is that I should find something that will make me smile because he says he hasn't seen me smile since I came here. And for the second task, he asked me to wish something for the New Year.

I guess both tasks have the same solution. I need to get as far away from here as possible. Not just the institute … but from home too.

I just need to be alone in a place that is unrelated to what happened. Maybe then I will know if I am sane or insane!

Because I feel like I was circling the drain and drowning when someone handed me a rope but didn't pull me to safety. So even though I am in a better position to handle what happened to me, I am still in the middle of the water. I am still very close to completely losing my mind. I just need to get away from here. I need to run and leave what happened behind me. I won't forget Lily, but I just want to forget the day I lost her … and how I lost her.

March 11, 2009

Jack was sitting in front of the lake, when John came and sat next to him.

"I was hoping to get you all better within six months of your admission, but you are not allowing me to help you at all. I now have to write a report on your case to keep you here another six months."

"But, I don't think I will do any better in the next six months. Why don't you just let me go home? I think I can get better there!" Jack said.

"I can't, Jack. It's not my decision alone whether you should stay or leave. I have to have a full case about you and judge whether or not you have improved since you came here. But you haven't been talking at all, and I hardly see you writing in your journal anymore. I had to change our sessions from daily to weekly, but still, you never talk whenever we meet. I see you talking a lot to other patients; do you at least talk with them about what happened?"

"No, I don't talk about myself much. I listen to what they want to say."

"But don't you think it is better for your case if you talked about what happened to you rather than hearing other people's problems?"

"No. I actually found that it is helping me a lot to talk to older people, who have been through more than I have. It's helping me cope better with what happened."

"So you still don't want to talk to me? This is the last chance before I write a report to request you stay another six months."

"I would really appreciate it if you let me go home this month, John. Please?"

"I am sorry, I can't do that if you are not responding to any treatments we are offering you."

"Okay. That's fair enough. But can I please ask you for a favour?"

"What is it?"

"Whenever Mom comes here to visit, can you please leave out the part where I don't attend any sessions? I just don't want her to worry."

"That's your call, Jack."

*****

April 29, 2009

Jack was in his room getting ready to go outside, when John came in.

"Hey, John," Jack greeted him. "I was just leaving to go sit outside."

"Jack, I need to have a word with you, and it is better if we talk here rather than outside."

"Sure. What is it?" Jack asked.

"One of our patients that you always talk to is a man who has been here for more than five years now and still refuses to talk. He even writes less and less in his journal every year. I have offered him many times to be a part of a research that I am carrying out, but he always refuses. Whenever I see other patients following the same pattern of behaviour as him, I always make them the same offer. So I'd like to make you the same offer; however, if you agree to be part of this research, then I will need someone from the outside to sign all the papers for you because legally, none of the patients in this institute can be held accountable for their actions and signatures."

"Before you go on about legal side of your research, why don't you tell me what the research is about?" Jack asked.

"Well, I have spent many years learning about the human memory, and I have carried out many successful non-invasive procedures that wiped out the memory of the subjects."

"Wait … So you get people to agree to wipe their own memories?"

"It may be difficult for you to understand, Jack, but many people are desperate for what I do. That is why I always need someone who knows my subjects from outside this institute to agree to the procedure so I know I am not the only who thinks this is the right decision for the patient. However, my rate of success is not 100 percent. But remember, that does not mean any serious risks or health complications for the patient. When I say my procedure has failed, I only mean that the patient still has all of their memories. And in some cases, my patients only lose their memory for few days and then recover it again. So this is why I try to carry out more procedures to try to understand more about the human memory. So I am here, Jack, because I am offering you the chance to be my next participant in this research."

"I really don't think I want to do this. I mean, I lost Lily and I may be having difficulty adjusting to the fact that she is really gone, but that doesn't mean I want to forget her and everything else that I did in my life."

"I was hoping you wouldn't refuse, but I will keep my offer open as long as you are here."

As John was about to turn around and walk away, Jack thought of something. "Wait, John."

"What is it?"

"How far are you in this research? I mean, are you able to choose what parts of the memory you can erase?"

"Unfortunately, I cannot decide which parts to target. The more I carry out procedures, the more I learn fascinating things about the human memory," John finished his sentence and walked out of the room.

The idea tempted Jack, and he stayed in his room all day thinking about it. But he still didn't want to give away all of his memories just to erase what had happened to Lily.

*****

From Jack's Journal
August 21, 2009

I can't believe it has been almost a year since I came here. John has finally agreed to let me go after I spent only a few sessions with him. I asked Mom to apply for a university course for me away from here. I am planning to stay at home only for few days before I move to my new city. John asked me once more to do a task for him. This time he wants me to list the things I have learned from my time here. He doesn't want to see that list; he only wants me to write them down for my own benefit.

I guess from the time I spent here, everything I have learned has been from the patients, not the doctors. The one thing I will never forget was something that was said by the man who has been here for six years and has never talked about what happened to him. He has never even shared his name with me, even after almost a year of me being here. He said, "No one suffers more than they can handle. We all face difficulties that take us to our maximum. So you should never go around claiming to have suffered extra or have been through more than others. Because if we are all suffering up to our own personal maximum, then we are all equal, even if the levels of pain are different."

He told me this because he said that through the time he spent here, he kept judging other patients on whether they were overreacting to what they had been through or if they were really suffering as much as they claimed. But the more time he spent here and the more he talked to other patients, the more he realised that there shouldn't be a set standard for suffering and pain. There shouldn't be a limit of overreaction because we all have our personal limits; some people commit suicide over their low grades in school and others over a cheating partner. While others go through life facing different difficulties every day and still continue to move forward because whatever they go through is still within their ability to withstand.

I guess he had a hidden reason for telling me this. Maybe he didn't want me to go back to my home thinking what happened to me was something huge and that I should always expect others to sympathise. People outside could have suffered more than me. So I guess I will leave what happened to me here in this place because here is where it really matters. Back in the outside world, people have their own troubles to deal with.

And if I tell them what happened to me, I will be putting myself in place of their judgments of whether I am overreacting or whether I really suffered up to my own personal maximum.

Home
September 17, 2009

Jack and Laura stood in front of their home, looking at the front door.

"Do you feel ready to go in?" Laura asked.

"Yes, I will be fine, Mom. I am much better now," he reassured her.

They entered the house, and they both went straight for the living room.

"I know you probably haven't had a good night's sleep in a year, so if you want to go rest, just let me know," Laura said.

"No, it's okay, I want to spend more time with you before I leave," Jack said.

"Have you still got your mind set on leaving? I mean, we can transfer your course here, and I can quit my job and stay at home all the time if you changed your mind and stayed with me," Laura asked in desperation.

"I know it will be difficult for you, but I really need to be away from this place. I think it will do me good," Jack said.

"I know you never change your mind once you are set on something, but I need you to understand that this past year has felt like hell for me. I was always used to someone being at home with me. And when your father passed away, I increased my hours at work just so I could stop my mind from thinking about him, but now I regret doing that because every moment that I spent at work, I could have spent it here with Lily. So, I guess all I am trying to say is that I don't want to be alone anymore, so if you ever change your mind, I will be here. And I wish you would come visit me every weekend. It's only two hours away."

"I will come visit you whenever I can, but unlike you, I really need to be alone for some time," Jack said.

"I guess I will just treasure these two days while you are here as much as I can. I have packed some bags for you, and I rented a flat near your university so you will be close to it."

"Thank you, but let's leave that for now. I am still staying two more days. Let's talk about something else. I spent all last year talking in sessions every day," Jack lied to Laura. "So I guess now I am ready to do some listening. Why don't you tell me more on how you have been feeling all this time alone?"

*****

From Jack's Journal
September 25, 2009

It has been almost a week since I came here. I feel like I don't belong in this place. If I didn't feel like I belonged at home, then how did I think it will be any better here?

I feel like I am someone from a parallel universe that has gotten stuck in this world. Everyone looks familiar, yet I always feel that I am the stranger. I sit in my lectures like a ghost in camouflage trying to merge into the surroundings.

Maybe the old man in the institute was right! Maybe people like us don't really belong in the outside world. Maybe reality is too real for us to survive in it.

I don't know how long I will be able to last here. Every day that passes feels like a whole year passing in slow motion. Will I have the will to go on here until I finish my degree? Or will I give up and run back to the institute, seeking sanctuary?

P.S. I left my home and went away just like I wanted, but I still can't bring myself to smile like I hoped.

Jack closed his journal and continued to drink his coffee.

The waitress came up to his table, smiling. "You have been coming here every night for a week, and you haven't said a word. And now you bring a journal and write in it? Are you planning on ever talking?" she asked.

"Well, I spent one year expressing myself through writing rather than talking, so I am no longer good at initiating a conversation," Jack answered.

The waitress sat down opposite him. "Okay then, let me start one instead. My name is Sarah. Are you new here? I have never seen you before except this week."

"My name is Jack. I arrived here last week to start my degree."

"So do you have any one here, any family or friends?" she asked.

"No, I don't have any family here, and as you may already know, I am not much of a talker to make new friends."

Sarah smiled. "Well, I don't work on weekends, so I am taking my little sister out tomorrow. Why don't you come with us? I will show you around, and at least you would have made a new friend."

"I really appreciate the offer, but I am going to take a rain cheque."

"Why not? Do you have any other plans, or are you just going to come here and write more in your journal? Come on. I won't take no for an answer!"

"Okay, I guess I have no choice."

"Meet me here around lunch time. I will bring Hailie, and we can spend the day together."

*****

Sarah and Hailie
September 26, 2009

Jack and Sarah met the next morning in front of the coffee shop where she worked. Sarah had a little girl standing next to her.

"Hey, Jack," Sarah greeted him. "This is Hailie, my little sister."

Jack knelt down on the ground and stared at Hailie.

"Is everything all right?" Sarah asked.

Jack stood up again. "Yes, everything is fine. She just reminded me of someone. But never mind."

"Okay then, let's go," Sarah said.

They spent the whole day taking Hailie to different places like the mall and the cinema until they finally reached a park. Hailie played with other kids while Jack and Sarah sat together.

"You are doing a great job being her older sister," Jack said.

"Yeah, she is my whole world." Sarah smiled.

"So where are your parents?" he asked.

"My mom died giving birth to Hailie, and my dad is as useless as the couch he sits on all day."

"Oh, I am sorry to hear about your mom. And I guess about your dad too. So do you study, or do you just work full time?"

"I don't study. I gave up on education few years back. I just work full time in the same place because I am planning to move out from my dad's place as soon as I can. I want to get my own place for just me and Hailie."

"So your dad really does nothing? He just sits all day on the couch?"

"Yes. He has always been like that, and my mom used to work all the time for us, but he never did anything. I am really surprised she stayed with him all that time."

"That's terrible."

"It's not all bad," Sarah said. "Whenever I come home sick of this life, I see Hailie smiling at me, and in her smile, I find the will to fight another day. She is the greatest sister in the world. She is so caring and mature for someone her age"

"I did notice that today, and she does have a beautiful smile that makes you forget all the troubles in the world. I noticed how she always tilts her head to the right when she smiles."

"Yeah, my mom used to smile the same way. So enough about me. What's your story? Why did you choose this city in particular to come and study?"

"Sarah, I am really sorry but I have been through a lot the past year and I still don't feel ready to talk about it yet. Please don't find it selfish of me not to share after you just shared a lot with me, but I promise you that one day, I will be able to tell you everything. I just need more time"

"I don't think it is selfish, because I already know that you are different. You know, I've never really met someone at work and asked them to come out with me and Hailie. I would never introduce Hailie to strangers. But I have been watching you for a week, and I can feel something different about you, but I can't quite seem to figure out what it is. So don't worry. I trust that one day you will close your journal and come talk to me instead."

Jack turned his face away. He didn't want her to see his eyes tearing up. "Thank you, Sarah. I really appreciate that."

*****

From Jack's Journal
September 27, 2009

Is it really possible, that in one day, your mentality can completely change and transform to a new way of looking at life?

On Friday I felt like I was a stranger from a parallel universe, but now I feel like I belong here. I feel that this is my world. And all this change happened after I spent yesterday with Sarah and Hailie. They somehow made me feel that my whole world has finally got a new centre that it can revolve around.

Sarah is a very special girl. The first time I saw her in the coffee shop, I watched her as she worked. I had never seen a girl as beautiful as her. But it wasn't her beauty that made me stare. It was something hidden behind her smile, something that was crying to tell her story.

I didn't know what it was, and it wasn't my place to ask. But when I spent the day with her yesterday, I knew what it was. She never complains, and she always puts on a smiley face just for Hailie's sake. That was why she came and talked to me in the coffee shop. She saw someone who didn't talk at all and always drifted away from reality. She saw in me what I saw in her.

And as for Hailie, when I saw her, I could have sworn she looked like Lily, but with curly brown hair. I knelt down to the ground, and I wanted to take her into my arms. But I didn't want to destroy what I have been building over the past year. Nevertheless, seeing the way Hailie looked at Sarah reminded me of how much I missed Lily, and it tore me apart knowing I couldn't hold Hailie in my arms just so I could feel what I felt when Lily used to run and jump into my embrace ...

For the first time ever, I felt like I didn't want to come back home. I wanted to stay with them longer. But when the time came, and I had no other choice but to say good-bye, I knew that I will be counting every minute until I see them again.

I really hope I can see them soon, and I hope even more that I can build up the power to tell Sarah what she wants to know.

P.S. I still haven't been able to smile.

November 13, 2009

Jack, Sarah, and Hailie were spending the day in a theme park.

Hailie ran towards Jack; she held his hand and pulled him.

"Jack, there is a place for pictures. They print them while you wait. Come with me. I want a picture with you."

Jack took her hand and went with her. When they arrived at the photo booth, she reached out with her hands.

"Can you pick me up and carry me on your back?" she asked.

"Yes, sure," Jack replied.

He put her on his shoulders and waited for the picture to be taken. Sarah watched Hailie and saw her smiling in a way she had never seen before.

"Jack, you and Hailie stay here while I go get some lunch," she said.

"Do you want me to go instead?" Jack asked.

"No, you got the tickets. I will get the lunch," she replied.

Jack sat in the corner and waited for Hailie to bring the printed picture. She came out of the booth with the picture. She sat on his lap, and as usual, she tilted her head to the right and smiled as she handed the picture to him. When he picked it up, he saw something written on it: *To the best brother in the world. Love, Hailie.*

Tears started to run down Jack's face. He smiled at Hailie, and Hailie couldn't help but gasp.

"Jack, are you smiling? Oh, I wish Sarah was here. She won't believe me if I told her I made you smile," she said.

"Hailie, do you really think of me that way?"

"Yes, I do. Every night I used to wish that I had an older brother. But the more time we spend with you, the less I feel the need to make that wish. Because I feel that somehow it has been granted."

Jack took her into his arms. "Oh, Hailie, I wish there was a way for me to explain to you how much this means to me."

"You don't have to explain, Jack. You are smiling for the first time in two months."

"Oh, it has been longer than two months. I haven't smiled in over a year!"

Sarah came back with their lunch; she found Hailie smiling.

"What's going on?" she asked but then noticed Jack smiling too.

"I made him smile," Hailie said.

"Now I am jealous. We had a bet which one of us would make you smile first, I guess I lost. What did you do to make him smile?"

"She gave me this," Jack said while handing over the picture to Sarah.

"That is a very beautiful picture. And it's very sweet of you, Hailie, to write this on it."

After they finished eating, they kept talking until Hailie fell asleep next to them.

"She looks exhausted." Jack said.

"She's had a long day! I have never seen her as happy as I saw her today." Sarah replied.

*****

From Jack's Journal
November 13, 2009

(Shortest entry found in Jack's Journal)

What else could I possibly have to say, after Hailie made me smile today?

December 18, 2009

Jack went to the coffee shop to see Sarah, but he didn't find her. He called her number but there was no answer. When he asked her friends at work about her, they told him that she called in sick.

He went over to her home and knocked on the front door. Hailie opened the door, when she saw him she smiled and hugged him.

"Hi Jack." She greeted him

"Hello Hailie, is Sarah okay?" Jack asked her.

"She has been in her room all day, I asked her many times if she is okay, but she keeps telling me not to worry and that everything is fine." Hailie replied.

"May I go up to see her please?" Jack asked.

Hailie let him in; he went up the stairs and knocked on Sarah's bedroom.

He opened the door slowly, what he saw next, was like a magical scene ... Sarah was sitting on her bed. She thought it was Hailie coming in, so she remained looking down at something that she was holding in her hand. Her hair was all turned to one side of her head as tears were slowly streaming down her face. A beam of sunlight was emerging from the window, breaking through her golden-brown hair and embracing her face.

Sarah finally noticed that it was Jack and called his name, but he was already drifting to another world. A world he has been warned about in the institute; a world of fantasy.

The part of his mind that used to take mental pictures of moments that he wanted to remember forever, was all of a sudden transformed into an artist. He wanted his mind to pause everything just so that it can paint a picture of Sarah and engrave it in his memory. He wanted it to use its finest brushes, to grasp the tiniest details of how beautiful she looked as she sat on her bed. When she looked at him, the beam of sunlight reflected on her blue eyes and made them look like shiny blue diamonds. And the tiny tears on her cheeks looked like sparkling crystals.

By the time his mind finished painting the picture, Jack had a little smile on his face. And by the time he came back to this world, he realised that Sarah was calling his name. She had been crying before he came, but after seeing him smiling, she smiled too.

*****

From Jack's Journal
December 19, 2009

(Longest entry found in Jack's Journal)

I haven't been writing in my journal as much as I used to before. Because the more time I spend with Sarah and Hailie, the less I feel the need to write.

Even though nothing will ever make me forget Lily, being around Hailie fills the emptiness that has been inside of me since Lily's death. And when I am around Sarah, my heart is excited by her presence alone. I feel like smiling every time she talks or moves or does anything.

Yesterday I went over to Sarah's house to check on her because I was told that she was sick and didn't make it to work. When I saw her in her room ... I really don't know what happened to me, and I can't find the words to describe it. I just drifted away to another world for what seemed like an eternity of one magical moment.

I didn't go blind, and I wasn't deaf, but I couldn't hear her calling me, and I couldn't see anything else in the room but her. My heart was racing so fast to a point where I hardly felt it beating anymore. Have I fallen in love? I wouldn't know, because what I felt yesterday was something that I never felt before. I guess all these years I have never really given any attention to any feelings I might have had because I was too busy caring for Lily. But now I think I may have fallen in love with Sarah from the moment she smiled to me in the coffee shop. The more I think about that moment, the more I realise how her infectious smile brought peace to my heart after a long year of conflicts in my mind.

I don't know how long was I looking at her as she sat on her bed. But I was so embarrassed when I finally came back to my senses and realised that she was looking back at me as I stared at her. I don't remember what excuse I made up but I changed the subject and went over to sit next to her on her bed and asked her if she was feeling any better.

Sarah was snowed under her troubles. She reached a point where everything was getting to her in her head. She wasn't really sick, but she didn't have the energy to make it to work.

We kept talking for hours about her dad and all about Hailie. We even planned how we were going to spend New Year's Eve together.

In the end, she asked me if I could stay over and if she could sleep while I lay next to her in bed. As soon as I told her that I didn't mind, she rested her head on my chest, and placed her ear right over my heart, then so quietly and so peacefully fell asleep.

I wrapped my arms around her and held her tightly till I fall asleep too. But I couldn't help staying awake, thinking about her ... and about everything she said to me. I needed to find a way to help her and Hailie.

I have only seen their father once, and it was more than enough time to understand what Sarah means when she talks about him. He is always drunk and acts violently. I fear for Hailie when she is around him because he easily loses his temper. I was once over at their house and was rehearsing with Hailie her part in a school's play. Their father came into the room and kept shouting and cursing and asked me to leave their house immediately. I felt so powerless; I had so much that I wanted to say back, but Sarah held my hand and asked me to leave before he gets any more violent. She explained to me why she doesn't report him to the police. She fears that once he is taken away, they might take Hailie away too and put her with another family in fear that she won't be taken care of if they left her in Sarah's care.

After hours of laying awake thinking, with Sarah sleeping in my arms, I finally came up with an idea. It's not all complete in my head, but I thought of taking some of the money that Dad left me. I can use that money to buy a small house, and ask Sarah and Hailie to come and live with me. If Sarah agrees, then I would be able to help them both live a better life than they are now with their father. And it will give Sarah the peace of mind that she has always wanted. She will no longer have to work full time, or worry every time her father drinks around Hailie.

Once I have everything planned in my head, I will tell my idea to Sarah, and hope she agrees to it. It may seem like a perfect timing to tell her that idea when we spend New Year's Eve together. Because this is the night that I am planning on telling her everything about me, about Lily, and how I really feel about her.

During our talk last night, we planned how we are going to spend New Year's Eve together. I will take Hailie out all day while Sarah finishes her shift at work, then I will bring Hailie home for her bedtime, and pick Sarah up to spend the rest of the evening with her until midnight.

December 31, 2009

Jack couldn't sleep all night. He stayed up for a reason that was unknown to him. He planned to buy some flowers for Sarah before he went to pick up Hailie the next day. So that morning, he went to the flowers shop and wandered around until the florist came and asked him, "Is there something in particular that you want?"

"Well, I want to give some flowers to my friend, but I really don't know which bouquet to give her," Jack replied.

"What do you want the flowers to say?"

"Pardon me?"

"Well, the colours are symbolic, so do you want the bouquet to say something or not?"

"I haven't really given it much thought, but she means a lot to me. She is really special," he said.

"Okay then, what is her favourite colour of roses?" the florist asked.

"She likes white roses, and I like red ones," Jack replied.

"Well then, that's perfect! What I can do is put a batch of twenty red roses in the middle as a circle and surround them with a row of ten white roses."

"That sounds good. Is that symbolic for something?"

"Of course! The red roses are known to represent love and affection. I will use them because you said she is very special to you. And as for the white roses, they represent purity and innocence. And the reason I am going to use them to surround the red ones, is because when you first referred to the girl, you referred to her as just a friend."

Jack smiled. "Okay, that sounds great!"

Jack thanked the florist, took the bouquet to his car, and drove to pick Hailie up. After he picked her up, he took her for lunch. Then they watched a movie, and finally, they came to same park where he had met with Sarah and her the first time.

He sat Hailie next to him and smiled at her. "Hailie, I've got a surprise for you, but you have to promise me you won't tell Sarah until I see her tonight."

Hailie smiled back. "Is it a present?"

"No, it's not a present," Jack replied.

"Okay, I promise I won't tell Sarah. So what is it?"

"How would you like it if I took you and Sarah to come and live with me?"

"Really, Jack? That would be amazing!" Hailie exclaimed. "We would be together the whole time. Sarah is going to be so happy when she hears this."

"Do you really think she will like the idea?" Jack asked.

"I think she will love the idea." Hailie stood up and hugged him, and then she whispered in his ear, "I know I shouldn't say anything, but Sarah really likes you. She talks about you all the time."

"You know, I really like her too. And tonight I am planning on telling her how much I like her. But you got to keep your promise and not tell her anything."

"I will, if you can promise me that you will take me wherever you go with her?"

Jack smiled again. "Don't worry. We will never leave you."

Sarah returned home as soon as she finished her shift at the coffee shop. She showered and started to get dressed.

Jack brought Hailie back home and took her up to her room to get ready for bedtime.

"Will you tell me tomorrow what you are going to tell Sarah tonight?" Hailie asked him.

"Yes, of course. I will tell you everything I tell Sarah. Now you should go to sleep early, and I will bring Sarah home as soon as we are finished talking. Okay?"

"Okay, Jack. I will see you tomorrow," Hailie said.

Jack kissed her between her eyes and left her to change her clothes to get ready for bedtime. He went downstairs to meet Sarah. He took her out to his car.

"So where are we going tonight?" Sarah asked.

"I've got some food in my car, and I found this perfect spot on a hill overlooking the whole city. We can sit on it while we eat and then watch all the fireworks that go off from the city," Jack told her.

"Sounds great!" she said.

Jack drove Sarah to the top of the hill and parked the car. He brought out the food and the flowers and placed them on a blanket. Sarah was too busy staring at the view to notice. She had never been up to that spot before. They then sat down on the blanket, and Jack gave her the flowers.

"Wow, red and white!" Sarah exclaimed. "They really look beautiful. Thank you, but what's the occasion?"

"There is more than one occasion, Sarah," Jack said. "I have a surprise for you that I am hoping you will like."

"Oh, really?" Sarah said. "What is it? No wait, before you tell me, I wanted to ask you how was your day with Hailie? Was she good, or did she cause you any trouble?"

"No, she was really good. I think she is really getting attached to me," he said.

"Yeah, I think so too. She really loves you. So what was the surprise?"

"Well, Sarah, there is not an easy way for me to explain to you what the past year has been like for me, but it all changed when I met both of you. I promised you before that I would slowly start talking to you instead of writing in the journal, so tonight I am going to start by telling you one thing, which is the root of everything in my journal."

Sarah smiled to him, "I would really like that. I have been waiting for you to share anything personal with me."

Jack looked down, then continued talking, "I had a little sister named Lily. She passed away last year, a few weeks before her seventh birthday, and I didn't really cope well with her death. I spent about a year in an institute, but I wasn't doing well with my sessions, and that is why they gave me the journal to write in whenever I didn't feel like talking."

Sarah's eyes filled with tears. "I am so sorry to hear that, Jack. But this already explains so much about you and the way you are so attached to Hailie."

"It's true; when I am around Hailie, she fills that part of me that is always missing Lily. And I've gotten so attached to her over the past couple of months that I really feel that she is my own little sister."

Jack paused for few seconds, and Sarah sensed him trying to build up the power to say something important to her. So she moved closer to him, and held his hand.

"There is something that I have wanted to talk about to anyone for a long time. It's slowly killing me from inside, and I can't take it anymore."

"You can tell me anything that is upsetting you, Jack." Sarah comforted him.

"The day I went to see Lily's body, I read a small piece of paper that had the cause of her death written on it. Since then I have been haunted with her image, and the memory of what happened to her. I have tried to forget what I read but I can't."

"It's okay, you can tell me ..." Sarah reassured him once more.

"She was only six-years-old when we were attacked. I was taking her to her first day at school. The thieves were only going to steal the car and take our belongings, until one of them took her and attacked her. The weight of her attacker on top of her body caused her ribcage to break from the pressure... and it punctured her heart and lungs. She must have been in an excruciating amount of pain before she died, and I can't...I just can't imagine how I couldn't be there to save her. But as soon as she stopped screaming, I stopped fighting back, as if my mind knew that the end of her screams meant that it was too late for me to fight anymore."

Jack started breathing heavily, he finally felt like a massive weight had been lifted off his chest. Sarah wrapped her arms around him and didn't say anything back for a moment. She knew he didn't need to hear anything from anyone as much as he wanted someone to listen to what he had to say.

"I am glad that you shared, but you have to know that I believe that this wasn't the end of your sister, I am sure she is in a better place now, just like my mom. We just can't see that place yet, and we can't hear them."

"I hope she could hear me, I hope she could forgive me."

"I am sure she doesn't even blame you for a second Jack, you did your best to save her, but sometimes no matter how hard we try, some bad things still happen to us. It's out of our control."

"Thank you for listening Sarah; you don't know how much that felt when I finally said it to someone."

"You can talk to me anytime you want; I am a very good listener." Sarah replied to him, as she unwrapped her hands from around him.

"There is one more thing that I wanted to tell you tonight." Jack added.

"What is it?"

"The time I spent the night in your room, I discovered how much you really mean to me. I found out that my feelings for you had been there the whole time since I first saw you, but I didn't give my heart a chance to express what it had to say."

Sarah blushed and tried to hide a little smile on her face.

Jack continued talking. "You may think you noticed me first in the coffee shop, but the truth is I noticed you before I even entered the coffee shop. I saw you through the window from the outside, and I noticed how you clearly stood out from the rest of the people around you. There was something different about you that made me enter. The reason I never felt this way before is that I spent all my life ignoring feelings I had because I was always putting Lily as my first priority. But now what I feel for you is something I can't ignore."

Sarah tried to avoid saying anything back that would interrupt him, so instead she took a sip of her drink and allowed him to resume.

"And since I saw how much you are sacrificing for Hailie, I have been trying to find a way to take some of the pressure off your shoulders. Maybe not even have to work full time anymore. So since you said you want to take Hailie and move out of your dad's place, I came up with an idea. I've got some money being transferred to me, and I want to buy a small house and ask you and Hailie to move in with me. But, Sarah, if you don't feel about me the way I feel about you, then please don't let that affect your decision to move in with me because we still have a great time together even if you think of me as just a friend, or even as family. So if you move in, we will always be together, you and Hailie will each have your separate rooms, and you wouldn't have to see your father anymore. So, what do you think?" Jack asked, hopeful.

"Jack, to be honest, I think the new house idea is really great, and I would love to take Hailie and move in with you," Sarah said. "And the truth is, when I first saw you, I felt something I never felt before too. That is why I started talking to you even though you never said a word to me. And just like you have a journal, I had a friend who I used to talk to before I met you. Her name was Annie and she works as a counsellor on a helpline service. But since I met you, I haven't been speaking to her at all because I am not as depressed as I was before I met you. But, you know when you said that when Lily was alive, you never really gave much attention to any feelings that you had because you were focusing on taking care of her?"

Jack nodded, as she continued "Well, I am in that stage now. Hailie has got my full attention. So as much as I want you and I to become more than just friends, I want you to be patient with me because I don't think it will be soon. So when we move in with you, I hope you can give me time to settle Hailie in before we talk about you and me being together."

Jack was about to reply to her when the fireworks went off above the city. The sound and the light caused by the fireworks distracted them both.

He smiled at her. "Happy New Year, Sarah."

"Thank you, Jack. Happy New Year to you too," Sarah said.

"Sarah, I know how much you love Hailie. So, I will wait by your side, and whenever you feel ready to give some attention to your feelings, I will be right here waiting for you."

Sarah couldn't hold back her tears of joy. She had gotten more than one surprise that night, and she didn't know which one she preferred most. She had gotten Jack to say something about himself after spending two months waiting patiently for him to share anything personal. She had finally gotten the chance to move out of her father's house and give Hailie a better life. And she now knew how Jack felt about her—the same way she felt about him.

Jack watched Sarah stare into the distance with a smile on her face and tears in her eyes. He couldn't resist smiling too because he knew her tears weren't tears of sadness. He placed his arm around her and looked out into the distance too.

"I love it when you make me smile, but it doesn't compare to the feeling I get when I know that you are smiling because of me."

*****

The Accident
January 1, 2010

Back in the house, Hailie couldn't fall asleep after they left her. She was too excited to know what Jack and Sarah would decide. She played around in her room to try to waste time. Just a little after midnight, she came out of her room wearing a white shirt, which she sleeps in, and a pink pyjama bottoms. She headed downstairs for a drink of water.

Her father was drunk on the couch. She didn't notice that he had a gun next to him, and she didn't know he had spent all day planning to take his own life. She ran in front of him, went into the kitchen, and stood in front of the sink to drink a glass of water. As she turned off the tap and raised the glass of water to her lips, she saw the shadow of her father approaching. He stopped directly behind her. She heard the sound of his breathing as it started to change. She was just about to drink, when she felt his hand touch her. The glass slipped from her hand, fell to the floor, and shattered into pieces.

Jack gave Sarah a lift back home around one o'clock in the morning. He stopped the car in front of her house. She turned to him.

"You don't know how much tonight meant to me. Thank you," Sarah said.

"Me too. You made me really happy when you agreed to my idea," Jack replied.

Sarah gave him a kiss on the cheek before she got out of the car and went into the house. Jack stayed in his car, watching her until she went inside. He continued smiling after she closed the door behind her. He was still thinking about every word he had said to her and every word she had said to him, when all of the sudden, he heard her scream once inside the house. Then there was silence. He came out of his car and ran towards the house. As soon as he entered, he saw Hailie half dressed, sitting on the stairs and crying. The ground floor of the house was dark, but there was some light coming from the top floor through the staircase, so he was still able to see that she was still wearing her white shirt, but no pyjama bottoms.

"Oh my God, Hailie," Jack said. "What is going on?"

Hailie's hands covered her face as she cried, but as soon as she heard his voice, she removed them and stared at him. After what was just done to her by her own father, she felt like she can't trust anyone, not even Jack. So there was a battle in her mind; she wasn't sure whether she should run to him and hide in his arms or if she should stay away and fear him. She stood up and started walking towards him as he approached her. She couldn't control her tears as she neared him. He knelt down on both his knees and opened his arms, but as soon as the tip of his fingers touched her shoulders, she jumped and ran towards the door, screaming.

Jack turned around and looked at her. "Hailie, it's okay. It's me. I won't hurt you, I promise. What's wrong?" She tried to talk, but she couldn't control her sobs. None of the words coming out of her mouth made any sense.

"Hailie, please stop crying and tell me what's wrong. Are you hurt?"

Jack started to approach her slowly once more, but as he did, she cried more and pushed her back against the door behind her. Suddenly her face froze, and she stared behind him. Jack still didn't know what she was doing. Just as he was about to ask her, her lips started shaking.

"Please … please not again," she whispered.

"Hailie, not again what?" Jack had barely finished his sentence, when her father hit him from behind with a lamp.

Hailie tried to run, but her father smacked her. She fell to the ground unconscious.

When Jack fell to the floor, her father pulled out a pocket knife and stabbed him in his left side. Hailie's father then picked something from the living room and went back upstairs.

Jack opened his eyes, he was in an enormous amount of pain and couldn't move. He turned his head and saw Hailie on the floor. Flashbacks rushed through his mind with the image of Lily lying on the floor between the team of paramedics; he even heard her cries and screams. He couldn't let this happen again! He won't surrender his mind to his body. He took a deep breath and decided to remove the knife out of his body. As he pulled it out of his side, he screamed. The pain was unbearable. As soon as the tip of the knife came out of his body, he screamed one last time and started crying. He then rolled on the floor and crawled towards Hailie. When he reached her, he brushed her hair away from her face, and in a low voice, he muttered, "Hailie. Hailie, please wake up."

He sat down, lifted her up, and held her in his arms.

"Please, God, not again … Please don't do this to me again. I don't want to lose her," Jack whispered.

As he was about to shake her softly so she would wake up, he noticed blood on her legs and thighs. He exploded into more tears, and squeezed her between his arms.

"No," he said. "It's happening all over again. Please, I can't lose her too!"

As he closed his eyes and held her tightly, he felt her heartbeat. He pulled out his phone and dialled the emergency number.

"Hello. What's your emergency?" the dispatcher answered.

"Please help." Jack said.

"Sir? What is it?"

"I can feel her heartbeat, but she is unconscious."

"Who is unconscious, and what happened to her?"

"Hailie. She is nine-years-old. She has been raped and knocked on the head. And I think she is still bleeding."

"Okay, sir. Stay with me on the line. Tell me your address so we can send someone right over. Just stay with her." After Jack gave out his address, the dispatcher asked, "Who did this to her?"

"It was her father."

"And is he still around?"

"Yes, he is upstairs," Jack said.

"Is there anyone upstairs who could be in danger?"

It was only then that Jack's mind was able to hear Sarah's cries. She had been screaming and crying since he had come inside, but his mind had been too focused on trying to help Hailie.

"*Yes*, yes there is. Sarah is up there. I need to go help her."

Jack dropped the phone and ran upstairs, ignoring the pain from his side.

"No, sir. Please stay with me on the line. Don't confront him! I am sending you the police as well as an ambulance. *Hello? Sir?*"

Jack reached Sarah's room, but it was locked. He hit the door over and over, but it wouldn't budge. "Sarah!" he shouted. "Sarah!"

He took a step back and gathered all his strength to kick the door, but before he could, a gunshot was fired.

In the following moment, he couldn't hear anything except his own breathing. His mind slowed everything down as he looked around, trying to figure out where the sound of the gunshot had come from.

"Sarah?" he called.

His voice started to change as his breathing grew heavier and more difficult. Pain blossomed in his chest. He pressed his hand against his chest and felt something. He held his hand out and saw it was covered in blood. Then he looked at the door in front of him, only to find a bullet hole. He realised then that he had been shot from the other side of the door.

His knife wound, the thought of Hailie unconscious downstairs, and the thought of Sarah in danger—all these things had been running through his mind so furiously that he hadn't even realised it. Now his mind could no longer resist surrendering to his body. His breathing grew louder and louder. He stepped back towards the wall behind him and collapsed to the floor.

With his last few remaining breaths, he imagined Lily wearing a white dress. She came and sat next to his head. He reached out to hold her hand, but he felt a transparent barrier between him and her.

She smiled at him, leaned forward, and whispered in his ear, "Not yet, Jack. It's not time."

She then kissed him on his forehead. Her image started to slowly fade away as his heartbeat started to slow down before finally reaching a complete stop.

Everything turned quite. Sarah's screams had stopped, and Jack was on the floor, not breathing. The police cars arrived in front of the house, but even with their sirens on, everything still seemed quite. Sarah and Hailie's father then turned the gun and shot himself.

The police officers signalled to each other as they moved cautiously towards the house. They then signalled to the paramedics not to approach the house until they deemed it safe and clear. First, four officers knocked down the main door and stormed inside the house. One of them knelt down to check Hailie on the floor, and the other three made sure the ground floor was clear. Two officers went up the stairs to check the next floor. They found Jack's body in front of a locked bedroom door. One checked the body as the other knocked down the locked door. They found the father shot in the head and Sarah tied to the bed by her wrists. She was awake but not responding.

*****

Emergency Department
January 1, 2010

As told by: Adam Jones – Head of the Emergency Department.

We usually have the same routine every New Year's Eve. During the early hours of the night, we get the usual minor accidents, then as the night progresses, the accidents become more serious as they become more related to irresponsible alcohol drinking. But that night was like none before. We never had three serious cases come in at once. I received a call from the emergency centre informing me that I should expect Jack, Sarah and Hailie and was told to anticipate them to be brought in by the ambulance team within ten minutes of the call. I had to prepare the best and the most experienced of my team to all be present and ready to take care of them when they arrived.

They were brought into the emergency department at three o'clock in the morning. Jack had been resuscitated more than once since the police had first found him not breathing. The ambulance workers had stabilised him every time, but his heart continued to give up and stop.

Sarah was in a state of shock; she was not crying, screaming, or even talking. Hailie had been crying since the paramedics woke her up back at the house. She refused to let anyone touch her and kept asking for Sarah. I ordered the doctors in the emergency department to give her a sedative so they could examine her.

January 1, 2010

Twelve hours later, Jack opened his eyes to a familiar voice. It was John, his doctor from the institute. "Jack, you are very lucky to be alive," John said.

"John? What are you doing here? Where are Hailie and Sarah?" Jack asked.

"They are okay. Don't worry about them now. I got a phone call in the middle of the night from the doctors here, and they told me everything that happened. My number is listed as an emergency contact for all my patients for one year after they leave the institute."

"So where are they? Sarah and Hailie?"

"They are in a different part of the hospital. I saw both of them and tried to talk to them for some time, but they are both refusing to talk. I tried to get Sarah to go and see Hailie, but she is refusing to move or be moved anywhere."

"Can I see them?"

"No, not now! You don't know how many times your heart stopped since last night."

"I need to see Hailie. I need to see how she is doing."

"I can tell you how she's doing. She is not doing well. She refuses to talk to anyone or do anything, and she is even refusing to eat. The doctors here are saying she will improve with time; however, from my professional opinion, her actions suggest she won't improve anytime soon."

"So what can we do for her? Do you know how to make her get better sooner?"

"If you and Sarah agree, I can transfer her to my own hospital, back to where you lived and went to the institute, and I can perform the procedure I told you about when you were in the institute. Remember?"

"Yes, your research on memory! So you can erase her memory as if nothing ever happened?"

"Yes, I can do it, but there is a 20 percent chance it won't work."

"So what happens if it fails?"

"Nothing. She will just wake up from the procedure with her full memory intact."

"So we won't lose anything by trying?" Jack asked, hopeful.

"No, nothing at all."

Jack drifted away into his thoughts. He thought about everything that had happened and how he could make it better for Sarah and Hailie.

"I am going to leave you to think about it," John said. "You need to stay in bed for few days. I will come back then to see what you have decided."

*****

January 7, 2010

After almost a week of bed rest, Jack got out of bed with the help of a nurse. She took him to the part of the hospital where Sarah and Hailie were staying. He stood outside Hailie's room and looked through the small window; she was sitting on her bed, and a nurse sat in the corner of the room.

Jack opened the door and went in slowly. Hailie didn't notice him. She was still looking down. The nurse stood up when Jack came in.

"I don't think it's a good idea for you to be here," she said.

"It's okay. I just need to check on her," Jack replied.

As soon as Hailie heard Jack's voice, she looked up and stared at him. She got out of bed and slowly walked towards him. He went down on his knees and opened his arms, just like he had the night of the accident. As she approached him, tears ran down her face. But as soon as his hands touched her shoulders, she screamed. She kicked him and pushed him away. Then she ran to the back of the room. Her nurse held her and tried to calm her down while Jack's nurse pulled him out of the room.

When Jack came out of the room, he was so upset by what happened. "Take me to Sarah now, please," he told his nurse.

"Jack, I need to take you back to your room," the nurse said.

"Look, please just take me to Sarah. Then I will go to my room," Jack insisted.

The nurse took Jack to Sarah's room. He stood outside it and saw Sarah sitting on her bed in the exact same way as Hailie had been sitting.

"Can you leave me alone with her for five minutes, please?"

"Of course, Jack, but I have to stay here outside in case anything happens."

Jack went into Sarah's room. When she saw him, her eyes started tearing up, but she didn't move out of her bed.

"Sarah, how are you doing now?" Jack asked.

Sarah didn't respond.

"Sarah, please. Talk to me! I need you to talk to me so I can tell you something important."

Sarah remained silent.

"I could really use your help deciding something. Can you please say anything?" he asked.

Sarah still said nothing.

"Okay, if you don't want to talk, then at least you will be able to hear what I have to say. There is a doctor that I know. He said he could do a procedure on Hailie that can erase her memory. It doesn't have any side effects, and it doesn't have any risks. He said if the procedure fails, then we wouldn't lose anything because failure only means that she will still have the same memories. I have just seen her, Sarah, and she is not doing well at all."

Sarah's eyes were tearing up as she looked the other way.

Jack continued "I think it will be a good idea to carry out the procedure. But I can't do it without your permission. After all, she is your sister. But if it was up to me alone, I would do it. I can't see her like this and not do anything about it." He paused and waited for her to say something. "Sarah, please. Say anything? The doctor is coming to see me today, and if I tell him that you agreed, we could do this procedure tomorrow morning, and Hailie won't remember anything. We could just tell her she had an accident and lost her memory. And you and I can go on giving her a better life like you always wanted."

Jack waited for Sarah to say something, but she remained silent. He turned around and was about to leave the room when he heard her voice. "Can you do it for me too?"

Jack turned back to her. "What?"

"Can you carry out this procedure on me too?" Sarah repeated.

"Why?" Jack asked.

"Because I don't want to remember what happened," she said.

"But I will need you to help me take care of Hailie after the procedure. If you lose your memory too, then how will I do it on my own? And what will I tell you when you wake up with no memory?"

"You will figure something out, Jack," Sarah said. "Please. Do it for me too."

"But, Sarah …," Jack protested.

"Do you know what it feels like when something terrible happens to someone you love and you feel that you could have done something to prevent it, but you didn't?" Sarah interrupted him. "Do you know how it felt when I saw her half dressed on the stairs and crying … knowing I could have been there to protect her?"

"Yes, I know exactly what it feels like. I lost Lily this exact same way. But I can't do this on my own. I need you by my side to help Hailie."

"Jack, if you really love me, then please do the procedure on me too. I don't want to remember anything that happened. I don't want to remember Hailie's face when I saw her crying on the stairs. I don't want to remember what was done to her, or to me. Please, Jack?"

Jack turned around and left her room without saying anything more to her. The nurse took him to his room, where he found John waiting inside.

"Jack, where were you?" John asked.

"Can you do two procedures on the same day instead of one?" Jack ignored his question.

"Why do you ask?"

"Sarah wants it done on her too."

"But Sarah is Hailie's sister. I was hoping she would take care of Hailie after the procedure. So if I do it on both, who will take care of them?"

"I will."

"How will you do that?"

"It doesn't matter now. I need you to tell me. Can you do the procedure on both of them as soon as possible or not?"

"Yes, I can transfer all three of you to my hospital tomorrow morning and do the procedure the day after. But I need all the legal documents signed, and you can't do this on your own. It doesn't work this way."

"John, please. Just this once, do the procedure with a verbal agreement. If something happens, I won't hold you responsible for anything. I just need to get this over with."

"What? Are you out of your mind? Do you know how long it took me to get my procedure approved? I can't do this without the legal papers. I could lose everything."

"No one has to know anything about it. I know someone who will be willing to help me out with all the paperwork. Just plan the transfer and the procedure, and leave the rest to me."

John turned around and headed towards the door. "If you don't hear from me tomorrow, don't blame me."

*****

January 8, 2010

John came the next morning to see Jack, but he didn't find him in his room. He asked the nurses about him, but they didn't know where he had gone. John went over to Sarah's room but still didn't find Jack. He went to Hailie's room where he finally found Jack sitting outside the room on the floor. Jack was holding the picture that Hailie had given him when they were in the theme park.

"What are you doing here?" John asked him.

"I couldn't sleep all night. I found this picture in my drawer next to my bed. The paramedics must have found it in my pocket the night of the accident, and placed it with the rest of my belongings."

John sat down next to Jack, and picked up the picture from him, he saw what Hailie had written at the bottom of it. "You know Jack; I never carry out my procedure on anyone, unless I am 100 percent certain that this is the right choice for them. And even then, I still get a member of their family to approve." John told him. "Yesterday I wasn't convinced 100 percent that it is even the right choice for Hailie. I have to admit, I came up with the idea to do the procedure on her because I was intrigued to see how the mind of a child will react to the procedure, as I have never carried it out on children before. But I still wasn't sure if I should go ahead with it. So the only reason I came back today, is because I saw how sure you were yesterday and I felt that you know what the right choice is for them. But now when I saw you sitting on the floor, I am not sure that you know what is right anymore."

"I don't know anything anymore. I feel that my mind can't take any of this anymore. I am very close to my limit, my maximum. I fear that soon I'll be buying the one-way ticket."

"What ticket?"

"To the world of insanity … Haven't you heard that word before, from the man I befriended in the institute?"

"Yes I have heard about the world of insanity and the world of fantasy."

"Well, I am afraid that the time will come where my mind will travel to either one of the two worlds, but I won't know it. I will still think that I am guarded by the great walls of sanity and reality. So how do I know when my mind has bought the one-way ticket? Because if I don't know what is right and what is wrong anymore, then how can I decide on the procedures?"

"Jack, listen to me; you said that you are close to your maximum. That means that you are still not there yet. So there is still a small gap left in your mind that can take a little bit more, right? So why don't you use it to make one final decision, and who knows: maybe when you make the right decision, and you become happy with it, then your mind will reset its limits, or even expand your maximum."

"And what if it doesn't?"

"I am your doctor, don't you think I will know whether your mind has travelled to another world or not? Now tell me, what was your plan? Maybe we can both convince each other what to do next."

"There is a man named Tom. He works in the police. He used to be friends with my dad before he died. I asked him to do a few favours for me regarding all the paperwork that we will need."

"And then what?"

"Then when Sarah and Hailie wake up from the procedure, I will tell them they lost their memories in a car accident and that we are family. I will take them to a house that we will buy in a small town far away from everything that happened to them and to me. Tom would have already taken all their belongings from their old home and moved them to the new house.

Sarah and Hailie were so excited that we were all going live together in one house like one family. So this is what I will do."

"Jack, this is not a good plan. This is very short-term," John said.

"This is the only plan, John!"

"If they were excited about it before what happened to them, maybe they will still want it. In both cases I have arranged for them to be transferred to my hospital to be under my care. But before we do the procedure, I want you to ask Sarah one more time, and if she still wants to go ahead with it, then everything will be set and ready for both procedures. The transportation is ready downstairs now, so we need to make a move. We may need to put Hailie to sleep for her own safety during the ride."

*****

January 9, 2010

Sarah was lying in her bed in John's hospital, waiting to be taken to the operation room, where the procedure will take place. Jack went into her room and sat next to her bed.

"Did you have any second thoughts about this?" Jack asked her.

"No, I still want to do this," Sarah insisted.

"Can you not sacrifice once more for Hailie?"

"Do you not want me to do this for Hailie or for you?"

"For me and her both, Sarah. I am not as strong as I was before ... I don't think I can do this on my own. I need you with me."

"I am sorry, Jack, but I don't want to go on living with the memory of what happened."

"I spent all night trying to come up with a way to say this that wouldn't sound selfish, but ... What about you and me Sarah? I love you, but you won't remember me after the procedure."

"And I love you too, Jack, but things didn't really turn out like we wanted them to. Please understand how much I need this. I have been refusing to see Hailie, or let her talk to me because I can't look her in the eyes. I won't be able to stand the guilt, even if she didn't blame me or judge me. I can't see her and remember that I couldn't be there to protect her."

Jack couldn't say anything back for a moment, until he finally replied, "If this is what you really want, then this is what we will do. But there is one thing I want. I know it will only make things harder on me, and I am sure that the last thing you want now is for someone to be so near you, so please forgive me for what I am about to do ..."

Jack leaned forward and kissed her; he closed his eyes and tried to forget everything, because he knew this would be the last time he would ever kiss her.

Sarah's body repulsed a little as soon as his lips touched hers; she didn't want any physical contact with anyone until she was over what happened to her. A tear ran down her face, when her body repulsed him. She never thought this would happen with Jack. But at the same time, she didn't stop him when he kissed her. She closed her eyes and tried to imagine that they are somewhere else. Because she didn't want this to be how their first kiss would be. She daydreamt about it a million times, but she never expected that this is how it will finally happen.

*****

The Hospital
January 10, 2010

Jack stood outside the room, where Sarah and Hailie had been kept after the procedures to erase their memories. John came and stood next to him.

"Are you ready, Jack?"

"Yes. Let's do this," Jack said.

They went into the room. John had two needles with him.

He moved to place the first in Hailie's IV.

"Okay, Jack, once she wakes up, there is no turning back in your story. Whatever you have chosen to tell them, stick with it." He injected the drug into Hailie's IV, and they waited for her to wake up.

She opened her eyes and looked at them strangely. She looked around her before she fixed her eyes on Jack.

"Where am I?" she asked.

Only now did Jack realise the extent of what he had done and the responsibility he now had to bear because of it. He looked at John and then back at Hailie. "You are in a hospital," he told her.

As Jack continued to answer Hailie's questions, his mind split into two parts: one judged him for what he had done and questioned whether he would be able to take care of them as if nothing had ever happened, and the other was thankful that the procedure had been successful and she couldn't remember what had happened to her.

When it was time to wake Sarah up, Jack couldn't stand the thought that she wouldn't remember him. His heart was rushing as John inserted the second needle in her IV. He stood impatiently as she slowly started to wake up. As she was just about to mutter a question, Jack couldn't wait any longer before he asked, "Do you remember anything? Do you know who I am?"

"No," Sarah replied.

He looked down and sighed; he didn't know whether he should be happy that the procedure has been a success or whether he should be sad that she will never remember him again.

*****

The next morning, Tom and Jack were talking outside the room while John answered Sarah and Hailie's questions inside their hospital room.

"I sorted out everything. The house, the bedrooms, and all the pictures," Tom told him.

"Thank you," Jack said. "You don't know how much I owe you for your help these two days."

"Don't worry about it; but please, you, me, and John need to sit down soon and talk about how you are going to make this work. You need a better long-term plan. I talked to the doctor earlier, and he was saying their minds are going to be in a very dangerous state. They are going to be vulnerable and paranoid at the same time. Their subconscious will be trying to tell them what happened, but because they have no memory of it, they will only end up with mixed feelings that have no story behind them. They will be very confused, scared and angry."

"Yes, sure. All I need is just few days for them to settle in. And if things start getting out of control, I may have to tell Sarah everything. I am assuming that since she won't remember what happened, she won't feel as bad as she did before the procedure. But I am only going to do that as our last option."

They went into the room and took Sarah and Hailie to the car so they could finally go to their new home.

*****

January 12, 2010

Just after midnight, Jack sat in his room, unable to sleep. He felt like something was not right. He felt as though something really bad was just waiting to happen. He went out of his room and slowly opened Sarah's door. She was soundly asleep. As he started to shut the door, she startled. She thought she was having a nightmare.

He went into Hailie's room and sat in the corner of the room. His mind played through everything that had happened to them. He wanted to sit and watch her sleep to reassure himself she was safe. But Hailie suddenly started screaming. He jumped up and ran towards her bed. Sarah hurried in from the hall. Together, they woke her up, and Hailie went to sleep next to Sarah.

Jack went back to his own room, but he was still unable to sleep. He brought out a box that he kept his journal in. He had some pictures of Lily in the box, along with some parts of the newspaper that had run the news of what happened to Lily and articles about what had happened to Hailie and Sarah.

He went through the pictures and newspaper clips and reminisced until morning. His phone rang and jolted him out of his thoughts.

"Hello, Jack," a man's voice greeted.

"Hello, John," Jack said.

"How is everything going with Sarah and Hailie?" John asked.

"Everything is fine," Jack said. "Hailie had a nightmare."

"Was it something from her memory?"

"I don't know. She said she doesn't remember it."

"I want you to keep an eye on her and see if she has any more nightmares. Sometimes the subconscious will try to jump start the mind to recover its memory through dreams. But, Jack, I am calling to ask you to keep any eye on something else."

"What is it?"

"Some of the nurses were telling me that up until yesterday, they still found some blood in Hailie's underwear from the attack. This shouldn't continue, but I need you to keep an eye on it because if it does continue, we might need to bring her back and refer her to a specialist."

"And how am I supposed to keep an eye on that, John?!"

"Just ask her if she notices any blood in her clothes, and if you can't, then tell Sarah to ask her."

The bedroom door suddenly opened, and Sarah came in. Jack hung up the phone and tried to put everything back in the box. But Sarah still managed to spot a picture of Lily. Jack tried to avoid her questions, but he couldn't avoid the fact that she was left feeling suspicious about what had really happened regarding the accident.

Later that morning, Sarah asked to have a word with him privately. They went to her room, and she started asking him more questions. He'd thought he had it all figured out until she asked him about their parents. How could he have forgotten to make up a story about their parents not being with them? He continued to make things up, but it was obvious to Sarah that he was lying. When Sarah walked out of the room, angry at Jack because he wasn't answering any of her questions, Jack noticed Hailie's clothes on the floor. He remembered he had to check them to let John know if she was still bleeding. He took her clothes and went into his room, but as soon as he entered, he heard the doorbell ring. "It must be Tom," he said to himself.

He went downstairs and asked to have a private word with Tom in his room. They went upstairs.

"I need to ask you for a favour," Jack said.

"What is it? Is everything all right?" Tom asked.

"I have a feeling that something bad is going to happen. I didn't sleep at all last night, and the last two times that I was sleepless for no reason, something bad ended up happening."

"Is there any reason why you feel that something bad will happen?" Tom asked.

"No, but I need your help. I need you to lend me your gun just in case something bad happens to us."

"What? Have you lost your mind? I can't give you my gun! Jack, I did everything you asked me for so far, but this I can't do. We have already done enough paperwork that could end us up in jail, so I can't add this too. I am sorry, Jack. I can't give it to you."

"But Tom, please? I was right twice before, and I am sure I am right this time too! Please, I can feel that something bad is going to happen. So please, just help me once more, and I promise you I won't ask you for anything else after that."

Tom pulled out his secondary gun and gave it to Jack. Jack took it from him and hid it with his journal in the box.

*****

January 13, 2010

The next night, Jack still couldn't sleep. In the middle of the night, he came out of his room and went into Sarah's room. He sat in a chair in the corner of the room and watched them both sleep. Something in his heart told him something bad was going to happen, but he didn't know what to expect.

The part of his mind that blamed him for everything that had happened to Lily was active once more. It asked him if he could have saved both Hailie and Sarah that night. He sat on the chair, thinking about everything that he could have done to prevent it all from happening.

Suddenly, Hailie woke up. She reached out to grab the bottle of water from the nightstand, when she noticed him in the corner of the room. "Is someone there?" she asked.

"Yes, baby. It's just me," Jack said. "Are you okay?"

"Yes, I am," Hailie said. "I was just having a dream. What are you doing here?"

Jack walked over and leaned next to the bed. "Do you remember the dream?" he asked.

"No, I don't …," she lied.

"Okay. Don't worry about it then. Just get back to sleep. You need the rest," he told her. "I may leave the house for few hours in the morning. If I do, can you and Sarah please not leave the house until I come back?"

"Yes, sure. We won't go anywhere."

Then Jack left their room and went into his own. He opened his box and took his journal and all the pictures out of it, leaving only the gun. He waited a few hours for morning to break before he left the house and headed for the train station.

*****

From Jack's Journal
January 13, 2010

Since I am on my way to give this journal away; I can't help but wonder ... Will I ever see it again?

I don't know if my constant feeling that something bad will happen, is all in my head due to the fact that I haven't slept since I agreed to Sarah's wish? Or have I been sleep deprived all this time, because deep down inside, I know that something bad is waiting to happen?

I don't know how I saw my plan as flawless. I don't know why I agreed to Sarah's wish or how I got John and Tom to agree and help me. I just feel like my mind was totally absent, yet I kept moving forward with this plan.

I guess I saw myself in her eyes. She didn't want to live with the memory of what happened. She didn't want guilt to build up in her heart and blame her for not being there for Hailie.

Maybe if Lily had survived her attack, I would have agreed to have the procedure done on me too so that her cries wouldn't haunt me forever. But because she died, I didn't want to lose my memory of her life.

I kept thinking all night ... What if something bad happened to me this time? What if it's my turn to follow Lily? Who would take care of Sarah and Hailie? Who would tell them everything? And what about Mom, who would explain to her everything that happened to me since I left her?

Maybe this journal can answer their questions. Maybe it will explain to Sarah and to Mom everything they need to know. But I haven't been writing much in it, and it won't have all of the answers! So after a long night of thinking, I came to a decision that I must give this to someone who didn't have a role in everything that happened. I am going to give this journal to the florist who helped me pick out Sarah's flowers on New Year's Eve.

But isn't selfish of me to gather all my troubles in one journal and dump it all on a stranger?

But it has to be a stranger ... She is the only one who had no role in everything that happened. And so no one would distrust her or disbelieve what she will have to say to them.

The more I think my time is coming to an end, the more I become scared of leaving everything behind hanging in the air, especially that I made a promise to Sarah, and now I am afraid I won't be able to keep my word. She may not remember, but I'll never forget. That right before they put her to sleep for the procedure, I whispered a promise in her ear that one day I would give her and Hailie a beautiful life.

But now that everything is falling apart, it seems I won't be able to live up to my promise. It seems that I won't have the chance to set things right. My only wish is that I can give them the life they deserve, even if I don't get to see it.

But if in the end, it wasn't my time follow Lily, then it means that the constant paranoia of something bad happening, insomnia and fear, are all signs that the great gates of sanity in my mind have been breached.

On his way back after meeting the florist, Jack received a phone call from Tom.

"Hello, Jack. Where are you now?"

"Hello, Tom. I am on a train heading back. Is there something wrong?"

"I will come pick you up from the station. I need to talk to you about Sarah and Hailie."

Tom picked up Jack from the train station, and they both headed home. When they entered the house, there was no sign or sound of Sarah or Hailie inside. They searched the rooms but didn't find them.

"Where could they have gone? I specifically told them not to leave when I am not with them," Jack wondered out loud.

"I am sure they are all right. It's a good chance for me to talk to you about them," Tom said. "I spoke to John today, and he explained to me how much Hailie is more likely to regain her memory through the dreams and nightmares that she is having. He explained how a child's mind can easily restore its memory much quicker than an adult's mind."

"What are you trying to tell me?" Jack asked.

"I am trying to tell you that if Hailie regains just a small part of her memory every time she sleeps, then she will be very confused and scared from the scattered pieces of memories that she will have. And it will be very difficult to help her. But if we tell her everything that happened, then she won't have any missing pieces from her memory, and we can help her better."

"What? Tom, how can you even say that? After all we have done to reach this point, you want to tell them what happened? So what was the point of this whole procedure then?"

"I didn't know back then that their subconscious will continue to try and grab their attention of what happened, even if they have no memory of it. Jack, Sarah and Hailie have a look in their eyes that they know something bad happened, and they are on a quest on finding it out. I am just saying we should tell them the easy way, instead of them finding it the hard way."

The door to the house opened, Sarah and Hailie came in. Jack asked them why they left without him and where they were. After Sarah excused herself and went upstairs, Jack asked Tom to leave him alone with Hailie, so Tom went into the kitchen to prepare some food for him and Jack. Hailie sat on the couch, while Jack came and sat on the floor opposite her. "How are you doing today?" Jack asked her.

"I am okay," she replied.

"Have you remembered anything from your nightmare and dream?"

"No."

Jack sensed from her short replies that she is trying to hide something from him.

"Hailie, right now, there is no one in this world that wants what's best for you more than I do. So if there is anything troubling you or upsetting you, then please tell me, and I will do whatever it takes to help you. So if you start remembering anything from your dreams and nightmares, don't let it build up inside of you. Come and talk to me and we will figure it out together. You may not remember this, but you and I were very close before your accident, and you used to tell me everything. So if there is anything that you want to talk about, just come and tell me, deal?"

"Deal," Hailie replied.

Sarah came down the stairs holding a gun. As she ordered Jack to move away from Hailie, Jack finally knew what his heart has been warning him about. He knew something bad will happen; he felt that he won't live for long.

Tom was in the kitchen preparing some food, when he heard a gun clicking in the living room. He peeked through the doorway and saw Sarah with a gun. He called his fellow officers in the station and told them someone was being held at gunpoint. He insisted that when they arrived, they shouldn't enter the house or try to take out the girl with the gun. He assured them he would try to calm the situation.

Back in the living room, Hailie ran next to Sarah. "Sarah, what are you doing?"

As the situation elevated, Tom kept signalling to Jack to tell them everything. But Jack was trying to leave this option as a last resort. But after he was accidently shot in leg by Sarah, he decided to tell her everything. He knew that he ran out of options. He knew that he can no longer protect them from the memories of what happened to them. As he slowly and painfully started explaining to Sarah what happened, he didn't notice that he was only making things worse. He broke down in more tears as he realised that this is the end that his heart feared. He kept wishing he could go back in time to make everything better for them like he always wanted. As he was about to continue and tell Sarah that he never hurt them, and never meant for it to end this way, Sarah shot him in his chest and he fell to the floor.

Sarah and Jack's eyes were locked; she thought he was trying to mumble something to her with his last breath. But in reality, Jack was imagining Lily sitting next to his head once more, just like he did the night of the accident. He looked at her as she stroked his head, "Is it time yet?"

*****

December 12, 2007

On the day that Jack's father passed away, Jack was sleeping on his bed, when Lily came into his room. She was wearing a white dress that Laura helped her put on. She came to Jack's bed, climbed on it, and sat next to his head. He didn't look too well, so she started stroking his hair, but he still didn't wake up. He didn't open his eyes, but he reached out and held her hand. She leaned forward and whispered in his ear, "It's time, Jack."

He opened his eyes, but he was very ill. "You were supposed to get ready so that you would come with me and daddy," she told him.

"I am really sorry Lily, why don't you go with Dad now, because I am not feeling well, so I can't come with you," he replied to her.

She gave him a kiss, climbed down the bed, and walked away. He kept watching her until she left the room, then he fell asleep again.

Because of this day that Jack kept imagining Lily whenever he came very close to dying. He was waiting for the moment when Lily can tell him once more that it is time for him to go away with her and their father.

*****

January 23, 2010

Ten days after the confrontation.

Jack arrived at his childhood home, but his mom's car wasn't parked outside the house. When he went inside, he found all her clothes on the floor. The kitchen was filled with dirty dishes. There was leftover food on the table that looked like it had been left there for days. Jack had never seen his mom like this; she always used to leave her home tidy. Jack went into her bedroom and found it was in the same state as the kitchen and living room. He took off his coat and started tidying up the house. He brought a laundry basket and began picking her clothes up from the floor.

At the same time, Laura was approaching the house. When she saw Jack's car parked in the driveway, she hurried to the house and opened the door. She couldn't believe he had come back. When she saw him, she stopped for a fraction of a second and then ran to him and wrapped her arms around him.

She started crying. "I can't believe you are back! How could you leave me alone all this time? I missed you so much. And I was so worried about you!"

"I am really sorry," Jack said, "but don't worry. I am not going anywhere anymore. From now on, I am staying right here with you."

Upon hearing these words, she sat down on the floor, still crying. "What happened with your studies? And with the house you bought? And how come you stopped calling me?"

Jack's voice started to reveal his bottled up emotions; it sounded like he wanted to cry and tell her everything, but he kept a straight face. "Don't worry about that for now. I will tell you everything. I am just really happy that I saw you, Mom. Why don't you go have a bath, and I will clear everything and make us something to eat?"

"You have always been caring, Jack. Ever since you were a child, we always thought you cared too much. Then when your father passed away, you doubled your attention to Lily. I never left you alone with her and came back to find her needing anything."

"You were the only two people I had left in this world. Of course I would have taken care of both of you," he said. "So now, why don't you go have a bath and relax, and I will tell you everything after we have something to eat."

Laura stood up, hugged him once more and then went into her room. Later that night, after they had dinner, they sat on the couch and watched homemade videos of Lily. Jack took the remote and stopped the video. He took a deep breath and started talking. He told Laura everything that had happened since he left her. He told her about Sarah and Hailie and about what had happened to them.

Laura cried many times while Jack told her everything. She checked all his wounds, and then she paused. "I am really happy to know you are okay, Jack, and that you sitting here in front of me. But do they still think you are dead? How could you let them live alone? Poor girls. I can't imagine how they are feeling right now. On top of all that has happened to them, they have no memory of it. They live alone in a house, and they know no one else in that town. They must be really scared."

"I didn't know what to do. After all we have been through, and after they started suspecting me and Tom had hurt them, I couldn't go back after I left the hospital."

"But Jack, Hailie is only nine-years-old. She doesn't understand all this. All she needs around her is comfort and security. Plus one week for us would be like a year for them because they have nothing else to do but to try and remember their lost memories. And they are going to be staying at home all the time because they are scared to deal with anyone."

After hours of arguing, Laura convinced Jack he had to take her to see them.

"Okay, okay, Mom. I will think about it. I am just glad to see you today, and we should go have some rest. We will continue talking about it tomorrow."

"But I really hope you think about the right choice for them," Laura said.

Jack stayed up, sitting on his bed for hours, thinking about what Laura had said. Then suddenly, he got up, picked up his car keys, and left.

*****

January 24, 2010

Hailie opened her eyes and found herself in strange surroundings. She was still sleeping next to Sarah, but they were in a different room filled with toys and pictures. She recognised the girl in the pictures—Lily. She knew her from the pictures Jack had kept in his journal. She was just about to wake Sarah up and ask her where they were, when she felt someone else sleeping on the other side of her. She turned around and saw Jack!

She didn't know what had happened. How is Jack still alive? She got out of bed and went outside the room. She saw a woman setting breakfast on a table.

"Hi, Hailie," the woman said. She approached her and hugged Hailie tightly. "I am Laura, Jack's mom. They brought you here in the middle of the night."

"They, who?" Hailie asked.

"Jack and Sarah."

"But how and when did they ...?"

"Don't worry about it, baby. Everything is going to be okay from now on. You and Sarah are going to be staying here. Jack went to the house last night and told Sarah everything, and he got her to agree to move in with us. They carried you and brought you, but you must have been too tired because you were asleep the whole time."

Jack and Sarah woke to the sound of Laura talking to Hailie.

"I am sorry, Sarah," Jack said. "I didn't mean to fall asleep here. Do you even remember what time we were up talking until?"

"It's okay. You fell asleep while I was still talking to you. It looked like you haven't had a good night's sleep in a long time. You cuddled Hailie and just drowned in your sleep. I didn't want to disturb you, so I left you there and slept on the other side."

They both left the bedroom and went to the living room. Laura came over and hugged Sarah. Jack hadn't seen his mom smiling like that since his father passed away.

"You know, Jack, I quit my job this morning," Laura said. "I don't want to work anymore. I have a new life to start with all of you here with me."

They all sat around the table and started to eat breakfast. After everything that had happened, there should have been some uncomfortable moments between them, but for some reason, there weren't any. If anyone had seen them from outside, he or she would have assumed they were one happy family having breakfast together. Maybe it was because every one of them had been holding on to the hope of being a part of a loving family, and so once they all felt the dream had come true, everything else didn't matter.

After breakfast, Jack was in his room, and Hailie came in.

"I am sorry, Jack," she apologised.

"Sorry for what, sweetheart?" he asked.

"I am sorry I didn't trust you and that I kicked you when I was in the hospital."

Jack froze. "Hailie … How do you remember that?"

"Every night, I used to dream about something different until it all just connected together in my mind, and now I feel that I never lost my memory."

"So you remember everything that happened?" Jack asked. *"Everything?"*

"Yes, I do, but I am not feeling as bad as I was before the procedure because all my memories now feel like dreams. So I do remember what happened to me, but I am not as scared or angry as I was before."

Jack picked her up and held her tightly. "Hailie, as much as I didn't want you to remember what happened to you, I must admit I am relieved you remember me from before the accident because I still feel that you and Sarah don't trust me. How about Sarah? Does she remember anything?"

"No, she doesn't remember anything. Even after she read the journal over and over again, she still can't get her memory back."

"Okay, I need to go talk to Sarah now."

Jack left his room and went into Lily's room, where Sarah was sitting. "Sarah, can I talk to you please?" he asked.

"Sure. What is it?" Sarah replied.

"Did you know Hailie remembers everything?"

"She mentioned that her dreams felt like memories, but she hasn't talked to me that much since last week," she said.

"So now that you know everything, Sarah, do you blame me for anything?" he asked.

"No, Jack. I don't remember how I convinced you, but I know I told you to erase mine too. I can imagine what I was feeling at that time. I was just trying to forget what happened to Hailie in whatever way possible, and when you came and told me about the procedure, I must have felt like you had come up with the magical solution. It was everything I wanted. It had the answers to all my thoughts—just one procedure to take everything away."

"I am really glad to know that, because I have been blaming myself this whole time for carrying out the procedure on both of you. Now come with me. There is someone I want you to see."

"Who?"

"Lily. I got some of her tapes out so we can watch them all together."

"Jack, wait." Sarah stopped. "There is something that I need to ask you."

"What is it?" he asked.

"As you know, I read the journal, so I know about you and me. Are you still in love with me?"

"Sarah, that's not something to talk about now. You shouldn't worry about me or about my feelings. I am just happy to see you and Hailie living with us here. That is all that matters now."

They went to the living room and sat on the couch with Laura and Hailie, and they all watched videos of Lily.

*****

From Jack's Journal
January 24, 2010

Last time I wrote here, I was feeling like something bad was going to happen. And I felt like I wouldn't get to see or write in this journal again. But I lived to see the journal and write in it once more.

I feel like if our life was a movie, then when we were all eating breakfast together at the table like one family, it would have been the time to end that movie, the time to roll the credits. To me, it was kind of a happy ending for everyone.

Hailie filled in the empty space Mom was feeling after she lost Lily. And Sarah and Hailie have found a loving parent to take care of them for once.

And me ... Well, I am just happy to see them all smiling again. Even though a part of me still believed me and Sarah would one day end up together, I am happy with how everything is now.

So maybe this is the time I should end this journal. I don't think I need to write in it anymore. Or maybe sometime in the future, something big will happen in my life, and I will want to write it somewhere. If that happens, I will write it here. But for now, this is how I am going to end it.

It's not a perfect ending for me, but it's definitely a happy one.

February 23, 2010

It was in the middle of the night, and Jack was in his room. He was asleep when he felt a gentle kiss on his lips. Then he smelled her scent. He couldn't be wrong. He couldn't be dreaming. It felt too real. This was definitely Sarah …

He opened his eyes and found her sitting in front of him on his bed, smiling. What a sight to wake up to. He hadn't seen her smiling that way in a long time. He was just about to ask her when she started talking.

"Jack, it wouldn't have been long before my heart would take over my mind and tell me that I love you," she said. "I may have lost my memory, but my feelings for you still remain the same, if not intensified. I kept thinking about myself and how I was before I lost my memory. I was trying to give Hailie a better life before I could give any attention to my feelings for you. So now that Hailie is happier than ever before, my heart is asking me to start giving attention to what I am feeling. And if my heart is correct, then you still love me too because every time you look at me, your eyes can't hide it. And now when I kissed you, something flashed in my mind, and I remembered our first kiss. And it made me smile, because somehow when I closed my eyes when you first kissed me, it got saved in my mind for me to remember it now and know how much you love me. But if this is not what you want, and you want me to leave, tell me. And if you still love me and you want me to stay, don't say anything back and let me just lie next to you and fall asleep with both my mind and my heart at peace for the first time in my life."

Jack's eyes filled with tears. He wrapped her in his arms and let her sleep next to him. She rested her head on his chest, placed her ear right over his heart and fell asleep to the rhythm of his heartbeat.

*****

From Jack's Journal
October 10, 2010

When I first started writing in this journal, I was lost for words. I didn't know how to start or what to write. My feeling is now mutual, but the situations are completely different.

I am lost for words today because I feel that my life is finally back on the right track. After all that we have been through, today Sarah and I are going to get married. This is not the best time for me to write in my journal, because the wedding is about to start. But I had to end one chapter of my life, before I let another one start. So since I no longer feel the need to write anymore, I will end this journal along with the chapter of my life that it represents. The reason I chose now to be the time to end this chapter of my life, is because most of the people that took part in it, are here today. So what better time to end this but now?

We invited Tom, John, and the florist, who finally told me her name was Catherine. We even invited Annie from the helpline because Sarah considered her as a best friend. Most importantly, I invited Elijah, the older man from the institute. The man who made me question every moment of my life since I met him;

whether I am driving on the road of sanity, or drifting away into the world of insanity.

Just watching all of them attend our wedding is making me smile because it makes me really think about everything we have been through in order to finally reach that point.

Hailie was upset at first that me and Sarah are going away on our honeymoon for a week. She reminded me of the promise I made her on New Year's Eve that we will never leave her.

But I'll make it up to her when we come back, by taking her and Mom away on a holiday.

We still don't want to move out. Hailie has settled into Lily's room, and Sarah and I will stay in my own room.

I guess I got a chance to keep my promise to Sarah, my promise that one day life would be beautiful for her and Hailie. And with that, the time has come to end this journal for good.

I can't help but think of something I learned in the institute: No one suffers more than they can handle. We all face difficulties that take us to our maximum. So you should never go around claiming to have suffered extra or have been through more than others. Because if we are all suffering up to our own personal maximum, then we are all equal, even if the levels of pain are different.

I kept on fighting, thinking that I am right on the edge of my limit. Little did I know, I still had a long way to go.

I wonder ... If I had known then that this is how it would all end, would I have still made the same choices? Would I have believed that we would finally have a perfect ending ... at least for now?

Lightning Source UK Ltd.
Milton Keynes UK
24 March 2011
169730UK00001B/35/P